TALES FROM
THE
BAYOU CITY

TALES FROM THE BAYOU CITY

A NOVEL

Tracy Daugherty

ZEROGRAM
PRESS
Los Angeles, 2023

First Zerogram Press Edition 2023

ZEROGRAM PRESS
1147 El Medio Ave.
Pacific Palisades, CA 90272
Email: info@zerogrampress.com
Website: www.zerogrampress.com

Distributed by Small Press United / Independent Publishers Group
(800) 888-4741 / www.ipgbook.com

Book Design by Creative Publishing Book Design

Publisher's Cataloging-in-Publication
(Provided by Cassidy Cataloguing Services, Inc.).

Names: Daugherty, Tracy, author.
Title: Tales from the Bayou City / Tracy Daugherty.
Description: First Zerogram Press edition. | Los Angeles : Zerogram Press, 2024.
Identifiers: ISBN: 978-1-953409-13-3
Subjects: LCSH: Folklorists--Texas--Houston--Fiction. | Immigrants --Texas--Houston--Fiction. | Minorities--Texas--Houston-- Fiction. | Blues musicians--Texas--Houston--Fiction. | Social classes--Texas--Houston--Fiction. | Houston (Tex.)--Race relations--Fiction.
Classification: LCC: PS3554.A85 T35 2024 | DDC: 813/.54--dc23

Printed in the United States of America

The town of Houston, situated at the head of navigation, on the west bank of Buffalo Bayou, is now for the first time brought to public notice because until now the proprietors were not ready to offer it to the public . . . [but] when the rich lands of this country shall be settled, a trade will flow to it, beyond all doubt, the great interior commercial emporium of Texas.

—Advertisement in US and European newspapers, 1836

The intercourse which [the citizens] have had with the world and with each other has had the tendency to [banish] bigotry and obliterate prejudices and most of them are able to estimate with little partiality the pretensions of all, according to their merits.

—Silas Dinsmore, early Houston settler

Contents

PART ONE: Low Rider, 1985   1

PART TWO: Comfort Me With Apples, 1990   33

PART THREE: Tombstone Television, 1995   89

PART FOUR: Burying the Blues, 2000   111

LOW RIDER
1985

1.

My name is George Palmer and my interest is insults. When I mentioned this to my wife on the day we met (she admitted later she disliked me at first) she said, "How come your parents didn't have any children?"

"I'm sorry?"

"That's an insult," said Jean. "Don't you get it?"

Actually, my field is insult *strategies*—social codes by which one group of people distinguishes itself at the expense of another. In Chaucer's day, for example, peasants told long humorous tales ridiculing landowners and lords. One of the most popular stories concerns a peasant commanded by an ogre to put his sheep to pasture. The peasant feigns stupidity and, by cutting off the sheep's tails and planting them in a field (as though the animals were head down in the dirt), pretends to bury the ogre's herd in the ground. The ogre believes his sheep have been slaughtered. The peasant sells the herd at market. With similar tricks he destroys the ogre's property, rapes the ogre's wife, and mutilates the monster himself. I told Jean, "I've got a good bedtime story in case we decide to have kids."

I'm rich. Oil money. Something Jean doesn't joke about. In 1941 my father and an Irish pal of his founded Ferguson-Palmer Oil in Midland-Odessa. Thirty thousand acres, wells producing

3

three hundred to twelve thousand barrels a day. In '52 my father left exploration, bought the company's refineries and moved to Houston where I was born. Our home was dominated by a ceiling-to-floor aquarium. A dark hallway led from the copper-paneled kitchen into a vast room, gently curved, the walls of which were made of three-inch glass. Muted blue light, languorous plants, soft living petals of purple and green. In recreating the Permian Period, when West Texas's major oil deposits formed, my father installed plastic brachiopods inside the tank and surrounded them with bass, catfish, rainbow trout. The room was his showpiece, his refuge from lawyers and accountants. When my parents were in bed I'd tiptoe down the hall, settle on a blanket in the flashing blue light, and let stripes of silver, orange and pink lull me to sleep.

As I watched the refinery workers from my father's office, my early awareness of insults grew. In front of the window he'd placed a bare table, a fence between him and the poisonous spires below. As a kid I crawled beneath the table, pressed my nose to the glass, and saw the men in hard hats stuck like spiders among the Xs, Rs and Os of the pipes. One would raise his fist, another grab his crotch. Bare asses were proffered. Shouting, shooting the finger. One afternoon I noticed a young Chicano slapping the left side of his face with the palm of his right hand. The gesture, meaningless to me, was having an extraordinary effect on another worker, who danced precariously on a catwalk thirty feet aboveground and threw his lunch sack into the air with rage. Years later I learned that the *cara dura*, indicating cheekiness or undue provocation, was a common put-down among Latins.

In thirty-two years of production, Palmer Refining logged over a hundred and seventy-five thousand Man-Safe Hours. "Our hydrocrackers are as tight as battleships," my father told me. Each section of the plant, roughly three hundred square meters of intersecting pipe, was color-coded according to steps in the refining process (red meant distilling, yellow purifying, etc.). State law required seven fireplugs painted the appropriate color

4

in each section. Sulfur and carbon, concentrated invisibly in the air, chipped holes in the parking lot, the workers' skin, and the paint, which had to be reapplied to the plugs every sixteen days: my first summer job. In my hard hat and jeans, turning orange, red then blue, I inhaled Lucite and steam until my nose ached. At the end of the day the workers bought me Lone Star longnecks and cold ham sandwiches. In the smoke and dusky light of the bar they reveled in being offensive. Their leathery arms snapped up in gestures of anger and fun, but my body was so sore from the day's work I couldn't enjoy the jokes. The waitress traded amiable insults with the man behind the bar ("Hey Numbnuts, I need a sloe screw." "Have to wait, Babe, till the end of my shift") but I didn't catch them all. I'd become aware of *hearing*—just as at the plant, sniffing its awful fumes, I was always conscious of breathing—and my head buzzed with pain. I swore I'd never work for my father again.

***

As a graduate student at Indiana University, the center of folklore studies in America, I edited a small quarterly called *Heartland Folktales* and dreamed of starting a press of my own someday. My mother, an education coordinator at the Houston Police Academy, supported my decision. "Do what you want," she told me one morning. "You're rich. What are you worried about?" I'd been out of school for a month and had come to ask her advice. She was relaxing on the police firing range between classes, pumping .38-caliber shells into the heart of a cardboard man. "You give a gun to a nineteen-year-old cop, send him to a one-room apartment in the middle of the night to stop a fistfight between a man and a woman, both drunk, who don't speak his language—*that's* worry. You, you're worth two, maybe three million dollars. What's the problem?"

Jean, a plasma physicist, forty-nine years old (and fifteen years my senior) always agreed: "I don't understand the point of your work, George, but if it makes you happy go ahead." I spent my days eating chili, drinking beer, editing manuscripts and writing essays on folk art for my Texas Republic Press, established in 1982 when my father gave me ten thousand dollars.

In the hair-curling humidity of Houston's hot afternoons I gladly went about my fieldwork. With a Sony portable cassette recorder whirring in my shirt I interviewed a retired postal worker who'd spent the last twenty-five years of his life erecting a monument to the orange. I talked to a woman who made plastic trees, lodging in their branches painted angels, Adam and Eve. I hung around with people on the margins of society, families visited by poverty and neglect: where folk art begins. If my subjects resented me for my privilege, my habit of sweeping into their lives to pluck their stories as curious objects of study (as some surely must have done), I never heard about it.

I spent a lot of time watching kids. I think children have always lived in America's margins. As Germaine Greer said, "Drinking and flirting, the principal expressions of adult festivity, are both inhibited by the presence of children." Kids' folk art, I began to see, includes astonishing insult strategies, as in their rhyming games ("Liar, Liar, Pants on Fire," etc.). Each morning I watched a redheaded boy named Steven, the youngest of the children in our neighborhood, scream as the older girls teased him:

Doctor Doctor can you tell
What will make poor Steven well
He is sick and going to die
That will make poor Lisa cry

Lisa Lisa don't you cry
He'll get better by and by
That's the sign he'll marry you.

Lisa was Steven's next-door neighbor, and nothing humiliated him more than having his name linked with hers, especially in singsong. The kids also established links through metaphor and simile: "Steven eats like a pig."

And direct statement: "Your father's a filthy plumber."

"Well, your dad's a midget Kung Fu spy!"

After lunch they often played leapfrog with Steven as "It." He bent down and the girls jumped over him. The oldest girl, a skinny brunette of about thirteen who seemed to be in charge, was the first to jump. As she did so she tweaked Steven's ear. On the second pass she pulled his hair. Next time around she gave him a little kick, and so on. If any of the other girls failed to follow the leader she had to be "It." I recognized the game as "Gentle Jack," first noted in Edmund Routledge's *Every Boy's Book*, first published in London in 1868.

"Possible topic," I scribbled in my notebook. "Steven, dismantlement of. His ego, his standing in the group . . . Playmates taking out on him what they often experience at the hands of adults?" The game, I noticed, had a strong verbal component, to justify the physical abuse: "You're a turd, Steven. Your mother's a mouse."

"Components of insult run deep, poss. in all lives & encounters," my notes went on. "Purpose of folk art to remind us? Purp. of children?"

2.

"I'm too old to raise a child," Jean insisted.

"It's still possible, though, isn't it?" I asked her one evening.

"You mean technically? Are all my cylinders still firing? Sure. But this fall I'm on the tenure committee, the curriculum committee, the executive committee." She taught at Rice. "Our peer review process for getting grants is breaking down in favor of congressional lobbying and *that's* a fight we don't want to lose. I don't have time, George. And you're out every night, God knows where, at your blues clubs or whatever. I don't think we'd be ideal parents."

She charged me with harboring an adolescent view of the world. "That's the trouble with poor little rich boys—sit around and dream, dream, dream. Sex, romance, the perfect little family. Daily life, George. It's stronger than anything. Dirty dishes, filling the car with gas, insurance bills, shopping for dinner." She kissed my ear. "Stronger, even, than all those eager pictures in your lovely young head."

In the fall of '85, when she found out I was having an affair, she tore me out of every photograph we had of us together. "This is the *vilest* of your insults," she said.

"I've fallen in love. I didn't mean to."

"Well, then."

"I'm sorry. I'd like to stay."

"With me?"

"Yes."

"Stop seeing her."

But—I'm ashamed to say—Kelly and I continued to meet. She'd walked into the press office one afternoon with a newsletter, *Update: Central America*. "The Refugees: Who Are They?" the headline read.

"Can you print a thousand copies of this?"

"We're not set up for that kind of work," I told her. She rubbed her long white neck.

This Woman: Who Is She? I thought.

"Sit down. Can I get you some coffee?"

She represented the Central American Task Force, she explained, a group of citizens ("mainly women—men don't seem as interested") concerned about the violence raging then in Guatemala, Nicaragua, and El Salvador, and US intervention in those countries—these were the high Reagan years. The Task Force shipped school supplies to San Salvador and seeds to Managua. They planned to leaflet every Wednesday in front of City Hall.

"Try Alphaset over on Richmond," I said. "They do bulk printing. They can probably get it out for you right away."

The following Wednesday at lunchtime I joined her on the street. Eight young to middle-aged women marched behind her in a circle, carrying placards: U.S. OUT OF NICARAGUA, HANDS OFF EL SALVADOR, NO PASARAN. Kelly, wearing a jeans skirt and a green blouse embossed with yellow parrot figures, handed newsletters to businessmen and women on their way to City Hall. "Get the hell out of here and stop disturbing the peace," a man told her. Kelly smiled. Conviction, controlled anger—a peppery combination, and it made me feel hot in my shirt.

She handed me a newsletter.

"Give me a stack. I'll help you pass them out."

Didn't miss a beat. "All right. You can work the crowd over there by the reflecting pool."

Four mounted policemen had cordoned off half a block for the small demonstration. "Whenever the Right Wingers march—the Klan or the anti-abortionists—the cops face the crowd so no one'll harm the marchers," Kelly told me later. "When *we* take to the streets they watch *us*, looking for excuses to break us up." Two men with long zoom lenses stood by a row of parking meters, aiming their cameras at us.

I offered a letter to a briefcase man. "Care for an update on Central America?"

"Fuck you," he said.

This happened three or four times. It was my fault: I couldn't keep a smile on my face. I understood their annoyance. Who likes solicitors? Once, I was standing in line at the Astrodome waiting to buy tickets to an Astros-Padres game. A militant farmer shoved a pamphlet into my hand. "If you eat you're involved in agriculture," he explained.

"If you throw up," I said, "you're no longer involved."

He snatched back the pamphlet he'd handed me.

"Commie bitches!" a man yelled now from the steps of City Hall.

Kelly kept her friends in line—they wanted to tackle him, tear him apart, ship him in a CARE package under cover of night to a tiny island nation porous with recent democracy, yellow fever and bent silver coins, massive market fluctuations and tsetse flies in the major export.

***

"So what does a folklorist do besides ask nosy questions and stick tape recorders into people's faces?" Kelly asked once the newsletters were gone. We were sitting in a coffee shop across the street from the courthouse.

"What makes you think we stick tape recorders in people's faces?"

"I took a class as an undergraduate."

"Not true. We're very benign. Not a peep as we go about our business."

"Which is?"

"Watching."

"Is that why you showed up today?"

"No. I wanted to help."

"What do you watch?" She crossed her stunning legs.

"Anything anyone does. The way you're sitting right now. The way we're talking. Culture's always changing. Folklorists try to capture traditions before they disappear."

"Like from old people, you mean?"

"Sometimes." I put sugar in my coffee.

"It's a bit anal retentive, isn't it? Regressive?"

"No, you learn all sorts of amazing things."

"Like what?"

"There are two kinds of old people."

"Oh?" She smiled.

"Sure. There's the well-informed old person, good as any library. Then there's the talker. The talker may not be accurate but the way he says what he says and the strength of his beliefs often tell more about the culture than any set of facts."

"When you get old you'll be a talker, right?"

"Why do you say that?"

"You came here to meet me, didn't you?"

"Yes."

"Do you have any interest in Central America? I mean *really*?"

"Of course." I ordered more cream. "They were taking pictures out there today—"

She waved her hand. "I've been photographed picketing the American Embassy in Managua. My file's a mile long."

In 1985, when this conversation took place, Nicaragua was the Left's cause célèbre—flying into a war zone a sign of status, like owning a compact disc player or a VCR. It's astonishing to me how quickly the Sandinistas (and the American Left, for that matter) dropped out of US news, swallowed by the fires of Eastern Europe and a leaky local economy, but back then everyone I knew had strong opinions about them, one way or another. President Reagan even suggested the Sandinistas might attack America, starting with the little town of Harlingen at Texas's southern tip. (There's nothing *in* Harlingen for soldiers to occupy, except a couple of damned old Dairy Queens.)

"This your first protest?" Kelly asked.

I nodded.

"Was it worth it?"

"You're interested in different cultures," I said. "I think you should come with me some night to hear the blues. I know the best clubs—Black joints you can't get in if you're white. But they know me."

"Are you asking me for a date?"

"I guess I am."

"I should tell you," she said. "I have two children from a previous marriage."

"I love children."

"Is there anything you should tell me?"

I slipped a napkin over my left hand but she'd already seen the ring. "I don't know," I said. "Like what?"

3.

"When are you going to work today?" Jean said.

"Soon as I get ready. Need anything at the store? I can stop off on my way home."

"Some Q-Tips. And a new ledger. We have to do the bills tonight."

"I wanted to stop by the lumberyard this evening."

"What lumberyard?"

"On 59. They're having a sale."

"What do you need lumber for?"

"I may want to build something."

She smoothed my thick brown hair and looked at me sadly. "What is it?" I said.

"You're not going to build anything."

"Yes I am."

"You always say you want to build something. You never do."

"Well, now I am."

"You have to pick bill night to finally get started?"

"No. It's just that they're having this sale—"

"Every time I ask you to do something, George, you've got some idiot plan in the works."

"The problem is you don't take me seriously."

13

She laughed. "No. Because your job involves going out every night and getting drunk."

"I'm doing research at those clubs. The blues are a dying tradition."

"If I ask you just this once to stay home with me tonight and help me with the bills, will you do it?"

"The sale'll be over tomorrow."

"George, I need to go over the Amex receipts with you. You have to be here, okay?"

Ah, the ogre's endless demands: "Pick the vermin out of my hair."

***

When the idea first occurred to me to customize a car I was sitting in the Elm Street Blues Club listening to a local zydeco band and splitting pitchers of Old Milwaukee with two guys I'd just met. We wrapped our arms around each other. "I'mone learn to play the pie-anny and join up with one of these-here bands," said the fellow on my left. He poked his red nose in my ear. "Make me a million bucks. Buy a brewery. And some beef."

"Hell, I'm going to *build* a piano," I said.

The other fellow was not a practiced scoundrel. I never did find out what brought him to the club that night in his three-piece Hart Schaffner & Marx, or why he felt compelled to join us in our joyful dissolution, but there he was, moon-eyed and slurry. He said, "I'm twenty-five years old, did you know that? It's a fact. And I'm going to tell you something. If I haven't made a million by the time I'm thirty I'm going to put a bullet through my head."

"There you go," said Red-Nose.

"And I'll tell you something else. I'm going to take as many people with me as I can." He made a pistol with his fingers and started picking couples off the dance floor. I poured him another glass.

"Get me a fancy car, or maybe an air-conditioned bus, painted up so's it glows in the dark," Red-Nose said. "Play ever' toilet in the South."

"That's it," said the Suit. "A custom-made Eldorado and an Uzi." He twirled in his chair, made a screeching sound like tires and aimed his arms at the band. "Chuka-chuka-chuka," he said.

I went home drunk, woke Jean up and told her I'd had a vision of zinc-plated hubcaps.

"George, those souped-up things are awful."

"It's folk art," I said.

Pots, pans, half-a-dozen eggs. Cajun food always sobered me up before going to bed, especially if I concocted a major mess, got to flinging spices around the kitchen. I pulled a red snapper out of the freezer, defrosted it in the microwave, dipped it in flour and milk along with a medium-sized soft-shell crab. Oregano, basil, cayenne pepper. A little Tabasco.

Usually in these late-night gourmet sessions, to keep myself alert, I mentally ran through as many blues labels as I could: Arhoolie out of El Cerrito (later from Berkeley), Alligator in Chicago, Memphis's famous Sun. Howlin' Wolf; Son Seals; Clifton Chenier, the Zydeco King from deep in the Louisiana Bayous. But tonight I kept picturing the car. I melted a pat of butter and saw in its golden bubbles shiny push-button door locks.

On Saturdays I sat in an unnamed café near the Ship Channel swilling Monte Alban from a bottle, imagining hubcap designs. Worms curled in the amber tequila, tugs moaned at the mouth of the bay. Dockhands wiped their fingers on the cotton stuffing spilling out of the booth seats and happily greeted one another: "Asshole!" "Pigdip!"

One Saturday afternoon a man at the end of the bar tried to teach a buddy of his how to eat crawfish: "Naw main, you gots to suck they little haids, like *iss!*"

Over time, a couple of Latinos from the refinery smoothed the way for me with old pros, young lions, and members of the gangs. With their help I built one of the classiest low riders in the city: crushed-velour dash, red silk roses wrapped around the tape player, velvet Virgin of Guadalupe in the back window. In the trunk, beveled mirrors, strobe lights, color postcards of the Astrodome, a fully stocked wet bar. A selection of magazines for my friends: *Time, Outlaw Biker, Architectural Digest*. Hydraulic pumps in the rear, lowered suspension in front. Tru-Spokes, "French-In" antenna.

Following Mexican custom I paid a priest from Maria de los Angeles Church in southwest Houston to christen the "Anti-Chrysler" (the odometer was stuck on 666,666). He flicked Holy Water from a cup onto the red vinyl roof.

"Excuse me, Father." I wiped a stray drop off the hood. "I just Simonized that."

The car would bring me closer to ethnic understanding, I thought: a passkey to the barrios. Or maybe I was just showing off. My wheels *did* provoke a few hostile reactions: "Look at White Boy there! White Boy tryin' to *ass*-immolate!"

I proudly displayed the Beast in every part of Latin Houston and was generally warmly received. In the northeast above Canal Street, Mexican families had opened groceries, *barbacoas*, funeral homes. The smell of smoked fajitas, lime-soaked onions and fresh tomatoes drifted past grassy yellow tool sheds and mixed with the aroma of coffee roasting at the Maxwell House plant over on Harrisburg. Even the wealthy families here lived poorly, ashamed of ostentation. Their Caribbean cousins rented modest brick homes in south Houston, near Martin Luther King Boulevard. I drove the Beast through these neighborhoods early one evening and made a lot of friends. Parched lawns, naked kids chasing the Paletas del Oasis, the Popsicle man whose tin-fendered truck played "Georgia on My Mind." Most of the Dominicans worked for Macon and Davis, on the nuclear plant north of town. On Sunday afternoons the men (full round faces, high cheekbones, coffee-colored skin) sat among saints and ceramic animals in their living rooms cheering Jose Cruz. "*He's rounding second, rounding third* . . . " In the kitchen, sausage and plantains, barefooted women chopping pineapples, whispering about the *tigres*, the "bad men" who demanded protection money from families in the neighborhood.

Koreans were now running most of the old Cuban markets, I noticed. The Cubans, getting poorer, were probably migrating to another part of town, but that wouldn't be clear for another couple of years.

Eighty to ninety thousand Salvadoran refugees lived wherever they could, anonymously in the suburbs or at shelters in Montrose and the Heights, partially gentrified neighborhoods where Kelly taught English twice a week.

"How'd you get involved with the refugees?" I asked her one night.

"Well, you can hardly grow up in Texas and not be aware of Latins," she said.

On Wednesdays she worked late at Casa Romero, the largest of the shelters. I'd fix dinner for her daughters, Monica, seven, Kate, five.

One night Monica pulled a deposit slip out of a drawer and drew an animal on it. "George, guess what this is."

"An ostrich."

"No."

"I can't guess, sweetie."

"Yes you can."

"Are those legs?"

"Uh-huh."

"A zebra."

"No!"

I put the cauliflower in the oven.

"Guess, George."

"*Monica*, I'm trying to make supper."

"Guess!"

"Okay, give me a hint."

"It lives in the water and has fins and long legs."

"I don't know."

"It's like a beaver."

"I give up."

"It's a beaver!" She laughed.

"Beavers don't have fins."

"Yes they do."

* * *

"Did you tuck the girls in?"

"Yeah. Kate's full of energy this evening." I kissed Kelly's breast.

"Wears me out."

"Are you sleepy?"

"I'm afraid I am. Long day. We had a fire at the Casa."

"You're kidding."

"Found some rags in the basement. Kerosene."

"Who'd want to burn the place?"

"Lots of folks. People in the neighborhood. There's some old guys who've lived there twenty, thirty years. They're real unhappy about all the Latins moving in. And the cops are always dropping by, waiting for us to provoke them."

"Anybody hurt?"

"No. We caught it before it did much damage, but life's getting spooky. Like those fundamentalist freaks blowing up abortion clinics."

I nuzzled her neck. On the wall above her bed, a world map: thumbtacks in every country from which she'd had a lover. "How many have there been?" I asked, pointing up there now.

"I'm not sure. I lost track somewhere down around Bolivia. How're things with Jean?"

"About the same."

"You could move in with me."

"I could."

She yawned. "I don't know why you married her, anyway. I mean, she's really really old, right?"

4.

Jean was working on a theory that the smallest particles in the brain—which she called "morphemes" in deference to my dumb grammarian's mind—were trapped fragments of the human psyche, just as matter was a form of trapped light. "Life is electrified activity in which every particle strives to return to pure energy, an unagitated state," she told me in bed one night. "The easiest way to do this is to attract one's opposite. This movement, of course, dooms each particle to solitude. If it finds its opposite, it dies. As long as it searches it remains unfulfilled. For every feeling of love there's a feeling of fear. These are physical, palpable things, George. I'm convinced of it. Fear *is* matter. And matter's free when it returns into light."

"I kind of like the shape it's taken here." I squeezed her thigh.

A glass skunk glimmered on a shelf above our bed. I loved that skunk. Jean had given it to me after a weekend tryst in Galveston—she'd bought it in a gift shop there—a year before we were married.

She lighted a candle and turned off the lamp. "Do I bore you with my theories?"

"No."

"One of the worst things about being nearly fifty years old is that life holds few surprises for you." She cupped herself around

19

my ass. "There's very little I feel excited about anymore. When I latch onto a new idea I tend to get carried away."

In the mornings she rose early and did fifty push-ups and fifty sit-ups. On Tuesdays at noon she had an aerobics class. In the evenings she liked to throw a softball around with me in the park. She'd developed a strong arm.

"I'll do everything," I said in the park late one afternoon, returning to my old subject. "Feeding, nurturing."

"Doesn't track with reality, bucko," she called back, whacking her mitt. "Babies just naturally go for the mother. They think we have the milk, even when we don't."

"It'd be different with an adopted child. They like a broader menu."

She fired a fastball at me.

"Ow."

"Even an adopted child would imprint on me. I'm just not willing to do it."

I watched Mustangs, Impalas and Gremlins shuttle by on the freeway down the hill from the park. On an overpass someone had painted "War Pigs in Space." A few miles away, helicopters lowered white stretchers onto a landing pad between the gleaming glass towers of the medical center.

Jean picked up the blue metallic baseball bat she'd brought. "Anyway, George, you need to decide if you're committed to this marriage before we start talking seriously about adopting a child. Because if we *do* have one then you run off with your little Leftie, that kid is your responsibility, not mine. I won't get stuck, at my age . . . " She tried to hit me a pop fly but the ball sailed over my head. "I *told* you you'd get tired of me. That day on the golf course, remember?" Hermann Park. The driving range. Neither of us were serious golfers but it was near Jean's work and it was a good, cheap place to hang. "I knew then why you were coming on so strong."

"I liked you."

"It was the novelty of seeing an old woman who could wear a pair of shorts."

"Jean—"

"You can't hang on to that beautiful young body of yours forever, you know? Golden belly, strong thighs—they're not yours to keep. You don't know what that means yet. Believe me, it's a shock."

"Let's go get some ice cream."

"Wake up one morning—"

"Okay? Jean?"

She started to cry. "My breasts sag, George! I have these handles on my hips! I told you that." She threw the ball in the dirt. "Why didn't you listen to me? Why didn't you leave me alone?"

5.

Kelly exhausted and drawn. Another fire at the Casa. They'd lost the whole kitchen and one of the downstairs bathrooms.

"I have to go back there," she said.

"It's after midnight."

"Can you stay with the girls?"

Monica and Kate were wide awake. I made some hot chocolate.

"Where's Mommy going?" Kate said.

"She has to take care of some business."

"George, remember when we saw the pony at the stable? With the brown spots on his back?"

"No, honey. I wasn't there."

"Yes you were."

"Your mother took you to the stable by herself."

"No she didn't."

"Did so." Monica shoved her sister.

"Snotty snotty snotty."

"That's enough, you two."

Kate grabbed my hand. "Remember his bulgy eye, George? Was his eye sticky?"

"I don't know, Kate. Probably."

She tugged my fingers.

"Yes, honey, what is it?" I said.

"Mommy says you live with another lady."

"That's right."

"Why?"

"Because she's my friend."

"Better friends than us?"

"Well. I've known her longer than you."

"My robot can turn into a truck. Want to see?"

"Okay."

"I don't like her," Kate said.

"You don't know her."

"When are you gonna live with us?"

"I don't know."

"I'll help you clean your room," Kate said.

"Thank you, sweetie. I appreciate that." I kissed her cheek.

"George?"

"Yes, Kate?"

"This lady?"

"Her name is Jean."

"She's like a grandmother, isn't she?"

"What has your mother been telling you?"

"She says she's about a hundred and fifty years old."

"Not yet."

Kate sat on her foot. "Does she have wrinkles on her butt?"

6.

Late one night three plainclothesmen arrested two Salvadoran women at Casa Romero and charged them with selling amphetamines.

"They were diet pills," Kelly told me afterward. "Laxatives. It's a war of nerves. They're trying to crack us bit by bit. They've subpoenaed our files."

"You've got nothing to hide."

"Well . . ."

"What?" I said.

"Harry, one of the volunteers here at the house . . . "

"Yes?"

"He made a couple of border runs."

"Jesus. Illegals?"

She nodded.

"You told me—"

"I know. But these were desperate people."

"How many trips *did* he make?"

"Three."

"The INS'll have a field day."

"I'll need you to babysit from time to time, but I think we'd better cool it, George, until things blow over. I don't want you getting mixed up in all this."

"Kelly—"

"I mean it."

She was firm. I knew I couldn't change her mind. I'd miss spending afternoons at the Casa. The place looked like a take-out barbecue joint—had, in fact, been a restaurant. A Pepsi-Cola bottle cap painted on the side of the house was starting to peel, smoky in the shade of four white oaks. Red cedar picnic tables sat in the front yard next to a gravel drive. Newspapers and old fliers, wrapped in rubber bands, nestled in the high wet, grass.

One day at the shelter I'd talked to a thin Salvadoran woman with dark scars on her arms. "Who did this to you?" I said.

"The *Guardia Civil* in San Salvador."

"Why?"

"They took my husband. I was passing his picture around in church."

The beige hall carpet smelled of cat pee and vomit. Wallpaper hung in strips. An old-fashioned dial telephone sat on a cardboard box in a corner.

I pulled a notebook out of my pocket. The woman rocked back and forth on the floor. "Tell me," I said.

"The men in masks, they force you to worship their whips, their fists. They give them names," she said. "'The Enforcer,' 'The Lollipop.'" She rubbed her arms. "After many beatings these words are the only ones left in your head. Your own name has been taken away from you. You've betrayed the names of your family and friends. Water hurts, light hurts, clothing hurts. But the hardest pain is not when they hit you. It's when they make you stand for many hours." She squeezed her legs. "Alone, in a room. You begin to hate your feet."

Water trickled through a pipe inside the wall. "The body—its own enemy?" I scribbled.

I recalled, as a kid, painting the fireplugs at my father's refinery: the soreness lingering for weeks in my back and arms, the weight of sitting and walking.

25

Insults to the body.

The woman closed her eyes. I thanked her for speaking to me. Her arm twitched a little but she didn't raise her head.

***

I followed Kelly's wishes and stayed away from the Casa. Most days I worked at the press or just drove around. One afternoon I went to the Shamrock Six, Houston's worst movie theater. I bought a ticket to a movie called *Hollywood Student Hookers*. I never knew in advance what was playing at the Shamrock or what time the films started. I came to watch the audience: predominantly Black, several generations bunched together in the seats—Great-grandad in the middle, Mom and Dad, festive kids spilling ice on the floor. Everyone talked to the screen.

"Don't go *in* there you fool, he waitin' for you!"

"*Now* you gonna get it."

"Yo ass be grass."

A circus of delicious put-downs.

Hollywood Student Hookers had been playing for half an hour. I took a sticky seat. Onscreen a woman shot a man in the face.

"I *tol'* you, sucker," someone yelled.

I sat through two showings of the film, greatly enjoying the crowd. Afterward I swung by Prince's for shakes to take to the girls.

Twice a week I babysat Monica and Kate while Kelly tutored her English students. One day I took the girls to the "Orange Show" on Houston's east side. That retired postman I'd interviewed had built a monument there to his favorite fruit, using scraps, pieces of farm equipment, and masonry tile. Winding metal staircases, red umbrellas, Texas flags. Stages for music and puppets. I loved to see the girls in my car, the way they sank into the seats like little dolls. Before we'd got in the Beast for this trip, Monica had cut the side of her foot on a sliver of glass in the street. Kleenex and tears.

"George, I'm bleeding on my shoe."

"It's all right, honey. Press down with the tissue."

Kate shot passing cars with a straw. "Our daddy was supposed to call us last night but he didn't," she said. She liked to comb the Chrysler's goatskin seats.

"George, *I can't walk*!"

"When we get there we'll get you a piece of ice to put on it."

Ten minutes later she was running up and down the metal stairs. It was late afternoon. A full moon low in the sky.

Watching the puppets, Kate leaned her small body against my back, resting her head on my shoulder, asking questions about the action onstage.

"What's that clown doing?"

"Reading."

"Reading what?"

"A letter from someone very far away."

"Farther than the end of the street?"

"Yes."

"Farther away than the moon?"

"Just about."

"Oh," she said, twisting around into my arms. "When will my daddy call?"

"I don't know, Kate." Kelly's ex was a traffic engineer in San Diego.

"I go see him in the summer."

"I know."

"We go swimming." She crawled off my lap.

"Hey," I said, pointing. I showed her the evening star.

7.

In the next three weeks, fourteen Salvadorans, eight Mexicans, and a Guatemalan boy were arrested at the Casa, on charges ranging from burglary and smuggling to possession of illegal substances. Casa Romero was ordered closed, its furniture impounded. Deportation proceedings began against nine of the Latins.

"I'm going to Arizona," Kelly told me one day soon after.

"What's in Arizona?"

"Harry has some friends there who're setting up a shelter. Desert community. Sympathetic to the cause."

I touched her knee. "Are there freeways in Arizona? I mean . . . I can't be happy unless I'm on a freeway."

"I know." She smiled at me sadly.

"You're sure?"

"Yes. I want to do this."

"Well, I'm . . . I'm going to miss you," I said, stunned, unable to think.

"Me too." She tried not to cry. "You're a real good talker, George."

***

Driving through the barrios, gazing at graffiti on old city walls: U.S. OUT OF GUATEMALA, U.S. OUT OF WESTERN EUROPE, U.S. OUT OF NORTH AMERICA.

A kid on a bike shot me the finger. I laughed. How could I leave this place, this seething gumbo of spicy, bad behavior? Houston was more than just the city in which I lived. It was a region whose intricate culture, whose social codes I'd cracked.

I called Kelly from a pay phone and told her I'd live on nothing but Fritos if she left. "I'll waste away . . . "

"You're being deliberately cruel," she said. "Come with me."

"What would *I* do in Arizona?"

"Open another press. Write books. I don't know, George."

"You think I don't have a life here. Is that it?"

"It's certainly not a life you can't improve on, is it? Is it?" she said. "Look at the hours you keep. The crap you eat. Here's a chance to start over, to lead an intelligent—"

"Intelligence has nothing to do with it," I said.

8.

When I thought about my children I imagined them in ten-pound, double-ply fertilizer sacks at the back of the garage. If I talked Jean into having them—a boy and a girl—I'd cut the bailing wire and let them out.

"You're late," she said. I'd been driving around all day. My eyes were swollen from crying. "Supper's in the fridge. Where've you been?"

"Running errands."

She'd been working on her computer. "George?"

"Yes?"

"How worried should I be?"

"What about?"

She looked at me.

I put my hands on her shoulders. She touched my fingers. "I don't know," I admitted.

She turned the desk lamp away from her face. "Maybe marriage loses its functionality after a certain point. What if it has a half-life of, say, five years?"

"What do you mean?"

"Probably people get married for very specific reasons. And when those expectations are met, or not, or when they're exhausted—"

"What did you need from me?" I asked.

"I wanted to feel sexy again."

I kissed the back of her neck.

"Do you know what quarks are?" she asked.

"Subatomic particles, right?"

"Do you know where the word comes from? *Finnegans Wake*. Guy who named them thought it was a nice-sounding nonsense word Joyce made up. Turns out, in German 'quark' means something like cottage cheese." She turned off the lamp. "I can't seem to make sense of—"

"Shhh."

Crying softly against my shoulder.

***

Kelly was leaving on Saturday night. "It's crazy to cross Texas in the heat," she said.

I nodded.

"We'll leave around nine. From the house. I hope you're there."

I squeezed her hands.

"You won't be, will you?

I didn't say anything. She kissed my cheek.

Saturday afternoon I drove for hours in the Beast, into the piney woods then south along the NASA road. I felt as groundless as an astronaut reeling in orbit.

Around six I stopped at a place I knew called Grady's and ordered a chicken-fried steak. On the bar TV the Mets were thrashing the Astros. I ordered a pitcher of beer. When the baseball game was over I played a little pool, threw some darts. Bought another pitcher.

***

Ten-twenty. My stomach tightened. *You asshole*, I thought. Maybe she'd waited. I could just head out, leave all my clothes . . . buy a pair of shorts down the road.

I was kidding myself. My mind had been set all along.

Mike, the bartender, said, "Rack 'em up, George. I'll give you a lesson in eight-ball."

I rubbed my eyes. Stood. Swayed. Jean would wonder where I was if I didn't phone soon. "All right," I said. Mike put a quarter in the table and the balls fell out: a thunderous boom.

"You break," Mike said.

"Sure."

We squared off across the room. Too much beer. The table swirled. Solids, stripes, slats in the floor, golden bottles, canned laughter from the television speaker. Mike shuffled his feet, waiting for me to move. "George?" he said. I chalked my cue, gazed at the tip. Bright blue dust rose into the air, shimmied, filtered down onto the smooth green table-carpet . . .

I remembered telling the girls stories at night to get them to sleep. I remembered sitting with them on the porch at Casa Romero talking to a young Salvadoran woman. Above us, cicadas caromed off the eaves. "They get in," the woman said, proud of her English, "when you open the door." I remembered trick-or-treating—Monica dressed as Madonna, singing "Like a Virgin," Kate wearing an Albert Einstein mask. She gripped my hand. "It was the scariest one in the store," she said.

PART TWO

COMFORT ME WITH APPLES
1990

1.

The Zamoras came to Houston from Jalisco, Mexico in 1988 and settled first on Hickory Street by a dried-up spit of Buffalo Bayou. Julio Zamora has never applied for a green card. He works as a fast-food cook. His oldest son, Manuel, loves the comic books I bring him every week. "Who's this?" he'll say.

"Spiderman. Tough *hombre*. He can eat fourteen burritos in eight minutes while hanging, half-asleep, on the wall."

"I can eat fifteen upside down!"

I think of him as my own little boy sometimes. He gives me as much pleasure as Monica and Kate used to do.

My other family, the Thuots, fled the Annamese Cordillera in what's now the Socialist Republic of Vietnam. They live with their six children in an efficiency apartment with no running water near Allen Parkway. I bring them food and job applications from convenience stores. They teach me their customs.

The Thuots and the Zamoras are precisely the kind of people no one—repeat, *no one*, *zero*, *zip*—wants to read about, Cal of Cal's Books is telling me now. He plants his hands on his dusty front counter. Next to the cash register a chipped fishbowl is gorged with slips of paper—a promotional gimmick. Cal's always got one going. Trips. Bonus prizes. At the end of the month he'll hold a raffle. Four free books.

"George, my customers want a peek at the secret lives of celebrities. Money, scandal, divorce," he says. "They're after books that'll teach them better love techniques."

Native American myths, Black oral histories, Cajun culture guides, Mexico, Asia—these subjects are Death, he says. Pure Death. Business is slow for my Texas Republic Press.

"At least take a look at what I've done here," I say. I've always been proud of the press, as its founder, publisher, and editor (early on, Jean suggested the logo, of which I'm very fond: an amiable armadillo branded with a big Lone Star). Today I'm the sales rep.

Cal takes my sample copy of *Houston's Latin Refugees*, a one-hundred page cultural study of families like the Zamoras. I'm also the writer.

"Sorry, George. I wouldn't be able to sell this."

"I can make the title less dry, less academic-sounding. *Tales from the Bayou City*. Something like that. What do you think?"

"If you could get me something sexy . . . "

"Be serious, Cal."

"Never more."

"All right, forget it." I glimpse an exterminator's truck back-firing as it rattles down the street. A giant foam rubber bug lies belly-up on its hood. Xs for eyes. It's followed by a pizza delivery van, pepperonis painted like measles spots on its dark purple doors.

Successful commerce: in the fast lane, way ahead of me.

I scribble my phone number and the names of the Thuots and the Zamoras on uneven ribbons of paper then press them into the fishbowl. Cal's got a picture of his teenage nephew, Ray, taped to the register as an ad for his "Family Novels" sale ("20% Off!").

I met Ray last summer when he worked part-time for Cal. He looks just like his uncle but neater, with a slender goatee. He said he was trying to save for his first car and to help with the family expenses. Cal told me his brother Billy—Ray's dad—was recovering from prostate surgery, something Ray couldn't talk about without choking up. I felt for the kid.

After that, whenever I came into the store, Ray greeted me warmly. Helpful. Polite. He always took time to glance through my pamphlets and books. He said he'd talk them up to his uncle. He loved showing me the latest issues of *Consumer Reports*, dog-earing pages of jazzy red sports cars he longed to get his mitts on.

A boy to make a daddy proud.

If I were speaking to *him* now instead of this old stick-in-the-mud, I might be making progress.

Well. Cal and I are used to each other.

"These people you talk to, George, they have, you know what I mean, kinky love practices, don't they? Fertility rites? Stuff like that?" His beard's about to wilt in the heat. "*That* I could use."

"Thanks for your time, Cal." I snatch back the book.

2.

The Zamoras live now near a Black college in the projects. Most families here are too poor to buy new shoes or to repair their old ones, and they have no sidewalks to use—only narrow dirt paths under splintered telephone poles near the street. The power lines between the poles are loosely strung over gardens and lawns, within easy reach of a child swinging a stick or a rusty baton or an old Louisville Slugger—something I'd fix right away if I had kids here. The fire hydrants, busted, are dry.

It's a ten-minute drive from Cal's. My air-conditioner's broken and I have to crack all the windows just to breathe. The Beast is no longer the Beast. I've stripped the car down so it's a normal Chrysler again. After about a year I finally got it through my head that a white boy tooling around like a Mexican hipster was an insult—and not in a good way—to the folks I was trying to befriend. Jean used to try to tell me this.

One thing about fieldwork: from time to time even a dullard like me can learn a thing or two.

The Zamoras' house is pink with dark green eaves. Spike cactus blooms on either side of the porch. A stiff plastic hose curls on a peg by the door. When I arrive Julio's trying to figure out the plumbing in his kitchen. He tells me he's just spent $780 on a new washer and dryer.

"Can I give you a hand?"

"Sure," he says. "Grab that wrench for me."

Some afternoons he cooks hamburgers at a Prince's Drive-In. Two nights a week he fries shrimp at a Chinese take-out on Wheeler. Eight months ago, he and his wife, Lira, and their five children lived in a small apartment in the Fourth Ward, behind a Southern Pacific railroad crossing. Now, with two jobs, he can afford to rent this place.

"Lira downtown?" I ask.

"Yeah. Pounding those fucking doors."

"No luck?"

"Nah. I tell her, she's gonna have to try a little harder. Small businesses, banks. Earn her keep around here." He laughs but there's a ripple in his throat. It's shallow and sad. Lira has been looking for work for a year. During that time, on at least two occasions, I've noticed bruises on her cheeks. Once, I couldn't be sure—she was heavily made-up—but she seemed to have a small black eye. She won't talk about herself.

"Every morning at eight she catches a Metro bus downtown and interviews all day," Julio explained to me once. "Then she comes home at seven to fix dinner for the children."

Last week I timed it and stopped by the house while Julio was still at work. I was hoping to get her to chat. A mistake. She was exhausted from the bus. The kids were hungry, hanging all over her—"Off!" she howled like someone in fatal distress. She pulled knives and spoons, pots and pans, from cupboards, cabinets, drawers. I asked her how she was doing.

She just smiled.

Right then, I wished I'd paid more attention to my mother as a kid. As a trainer at the police academy, her job was to walk young cops through hypothetical situations they might encounter in the field, including the kind of domestic squalor I faced down now. But I couldn't recall a single thing my mother ever said that would help me with Lira.

I told her my friend Cal had some new employment guides in his bookstore. She said she'd check them out. Then politely, "Excuse me."

"Sure," I said, and left as quickly as I could.

Now, as Julio and I hammer beneath the sink, Manuel, his eight-year-old, active as a beetle, sings into my portable tape recorder:

No llores, Jesus, no llores
Que nos vos a hacer llorar.
Pues los niños de este pueblo
Te queremos consolar.

Julio laughs. "What a morbid little song! *No Llores*," he says, "is a funeral dirge."

I pull a pencil from my pocket and jot that down.

Years ago, in an informal study when I started the press, I discovered that white Houston tended to stereotype Mexicans according to their food behavior: "Greaser," "Pepper-belly," "Frijoles-guzzler." It occurs to me to ask Julio his names for *norteños*.

After the washer's hooked up in the pantry Julio opens a plastic tub of salsa and a bag of tortilla chips and sets them on his rickety kitchen table. Manuel listens to the Astros on the radio.

The house is packed to its peeling pine rafters with keepsakes, toys, pages of jubilant scribbles by the kids, the sweet-and-sour smells of brimming life—gifts I expected to gather myself someday, I think.

"Okay, how do we start?" Julio says.

I fumble the recorder. Why do my hands shake? I seem to have been rattled by the kids' fanciful drawings. "Well," I say, switching the recorder on. "Today let's talk about insults, okay? Do you have, you know, derogatory terms for Anglos?"

He thinks for a minute. "Yes. Sometimes we call you *Jamónes*."

"What does it mean?"

"Ham-eaters. You know, you're big eaters of pork."

"What else?"

"*Bolillo*, Rolling Pin. Because of the way you move, I guess: straight-ahead, arrogant. I never really knew. It's just something I heard from my father. He used to tell us stories at night—big man, dark like an African. He taught me nothing is more important than family."

I nod.

"*Niňo*, family, it's the solid rock of life, he used to say." He laughs and gestures at the blinking red light on my machine. "So. This will be another book?"

"Maybe part of one," I say. "I don't know. I'm running out of money." (Something I never thought I'd face.)

He surprises me by grasping my knee. He's always surprising me, switching gears—happy to sad, wistful to tough. In all our many talks, I've yet to learn how to read him. "Whatever happens, don't quit, George. It's a good thing you're doing, telling our stories to the Anglos."

"I appreciate it. Not everyone feels that way."

"Why not?"

"You know, they see me as a man of privilege, stepping in . . . exploiting your culture, stealing your voice . . . "

"Ah hell. If you didn't get this stuff out, it wouldn't get out at all. It ain't gonna come from us. I mean, look around."

"Oh, I don't know. With the right opportunities . . . "

"Like I said. Look around."

Suddenly I'm exhausted. I rub my eyes. Before my *zero*, my *zip* with Cal today, I logged eight and half hours at the newspaper.

"Ah, you're beat," Julio says. "We should quit, eh? You need to go home and let your lady fix you a nice supper."

Children shout, playing tag down the street.

"Right. If I *had* a lady," I mutter. And there it is: my salty, slippery grief, spoken aloud for the first time in months.

"A nice-lookin' fellow like you? No lady?"

My hands tremble again. I almost tell him, "The freeway ate her up, man. Swallowed her whole." But he doesn't need to

41

know this. His world's cluttered already: washers, dryers, faint black bruises.

"Anglos." He *tsks*. "Always too busy for love. You don't know how to appreciate a good woman."

"You're right," I say, and now, instead of Jean, I flash on Kelly. She still haunts me after all these years, a pleasant ghost, but a ghost nonetheless. For a while she kept in touch. Then her letters stopped coming. She'd found a new man, she said. She was happy. She'd settled near Ajo, Arizona. She'd joined a group dedicated to leaving jugs of water for migrants trudging through the brutal Sonoran Desert. The girls were becoming little monsters, she said in her last card: sullen pre-adolescents.

I glance again at the kids' drawings on Julio's table and try to steady my hands. For me, Monica and Kate will always be seven and five.

"Sometimes when I see white folks dance, I think, 'How can they be so clumsy with their bodies and still make babies?'" Julio says.

I try to laugh.

"No, really. It makes me very sad."

As I'm leaving a few minutes later, I see Lira at the end of the block stepping from a steaming silver bus. She grips a grocery bag. I wave through the windshield of my car but she doesn't see me. Her eyes are fixed on her own front door—a wide, cautious stare as though she's keeping tabs on a rabid animal. She's lovely, a deep, rich brown, her bare arms slightly muscled, her blouse and green skirt neat despite what I imagine to be the hardships of her day and the indignity of pressing bus crowds.

What could I offer her? Proofreader? Editorial assistant? No. I can't afford to hire anyone.

I wave again. She still hasn't noticed my car's slow turning. Julio's waiting now in the open doorway. Her pace quickens. She tightens her grasp on the bag and it tears at the bottom, spilling eggs and milk.

3.

My weekly visits with the Thuots are usually tenser than my sessions with Julio Zamora.

A year ago, when I met them, they stood with their arms folded and gave me a very wide berth. Later, a fellow folklorist told me that in most Asian cultures folding one's arms is a gesture of honor. Distance signals respect. In time, the Thuots sang into my tape recorder, shared stories and jokes. They showed me bracelets they'd made from American artillery scraps.

Mr. Thuot is stooped, wrinkled and dark. His wife is tall with slender, peach-colored ears. They have four boys and two girls, none of them getting an education at the moment, though three of the boys are old enough for high school. Their apartment overlooks a deep part of the bayou. Beyond it, the rice mills of American Grain, gleaming white, tall as rockets.

The family bathes in water from the stream. Mr. Thuot and the boys haul it in buckets to a giant steel tub in the center of their living room. I've told them the bayou's polluted—I've seen car doors, portable freezers, bicycle mirrors rusting in the mud. The Thuots always drink the fresh Ozarka water I bring them, shear the plastic bottles in half and use them to carry dirty bathwater up the banks.

Tonight the streets are muggy and hot. A steamy film clings to the bayou's surface.

I hand Mr. Thuot a stack of applications for employment—gas stations, grocery stores—saving some for Lira Zamora. My nerves have settled since leaving Julio's place. My hands no longer shake. Still, I'm eager to finish my business, head downtown, deal poker with my office mates and get my mind off myself tonight.

"Thank you," Mr. Thuot says, folding the applications into his back pocket. No smile.

He sits on his couch, back straight, waiting for me to turn on my Sony. His wife sits beside him. Her hair smells like lilacs. "We don't have to do this," I say, sensing Mr. Thuot's mood.

Curtly, he nods, waves his hands. His English is good. I love his family stories.

I'm the bearer, now, of other families' stories.

"You want more about my birthplace?" he asks. "My—how do you put it?—my 'origin'?"

"What haven't we covered so far?"

"Grandfather. Distant cousins. Yes?" He offers me green tea, hands me a blue dish with slices of orange.

Last August, on my first visit, I learned that his home village, Kontum, a series of bamboo huts on the Annam Cordillera highlands, was a lush, fertile place, brimming with kids. Mr. Thuot had been a farmer and a fisherman. The streams were treacherous, full of crocodiles, so for luck he'd tattooed a green snake on his chest (a folk practice I've traced to the fourteenth century).

On that same visit, Mrs. Thuot told me that in the mountains, married couples often whispered sibling terms—"Yes, my brother, yes, yes!"—while making love, a practice common also in Thailand.

"How about this instead," I tell Mr. Thuot now. "It's a little delicate, and not to get too personal, but . . . would you mind sharing with me some of the intimate words for the pleasures you feel with your wife? It's of cultural interest."

As I speak I watch the tape roll inside my recorder. It's like my clattery mind looping back to Jean: her small, puckered mouth trying to tell me something.

Mr. Thuot trusts me and enjoys our talks but he seems, this evening, grim. The tape hisses and we avoid each other's eyes. Finally, I turn off the little machine and start to leave.

Mrs. Thuot, worried that her husband has offended me, motions for me to sit back down. Her primary domestic duty, as far as I've been able to tell, is to sweep unpleasantness out of her home. She rummages in a battered trunk full of keepsakes, pulling out three small gongs: metal with upturned rims. Excitedly, she gestures for her husband to explain.

"He is not interested—"

"Yes," I say. "I am. Please."

Delicately, he touches each gong. "These we use on several occasions," he says. "Funerals, feasts. We had many gongs but three was all we could pack, fleeing the war. The largest is called *Knah*. Part of a set of six. When they are stored together, one inside the other, they form concentric circles. The smaller gongs are *Ching*. They come in sets of three. We use at family dinner."

Mrs. Thuot mimes the picking of chopsticks. I laugh and join her. Mr. Thuot smiles, raises his glass of tea—"To the children," he toasts, "to the high sky of their future, yes?"—and with his long yellow nails taps the tiny *Ching*.

Later, as I'm preparing to leave, Mrs. Thuot tells me, "A family vanished here last night." We're standing in a vacant lot behind her apartment next to my dusty Chrysler. "Right over there. That one." She points to an unpainted door in the building beside hers. "This is why my husband is distracted for you today." Her eyes mist.

In this part of town, "vanished" could mean anything. Deported. Chased away by crack dealers, Chicano gangs, Black gangs, white gangs, Asian gangs. Shot to death.

"It scares me," she says.

"Yes."

As if to accentuate her thought, a car squeals its tires in the darkness down by the bayou.

I ask her, "Do you have everything you need right now?"

She smiles. "Who can tell?" she says. She squeezes my hand. "People need so much."

4.

M y family vanished a year ago on the Gulf Coast Freeway.
"Freak," said the first officer on the scene. In my daze, I
thought he meant me for surviving, and I agreed with him. "No,
no." He draped his arm around my shoulder. "I meant the accident."

All I remember of the instant before my world changed is
a candy-red pickup veering into our lane: lawn mowers, trash
barrels, rakes in its bed. Then I'm standing by the road in the
hot, sucking wind of cars going past, giving the officer my name.

This is what I couldn't tell Julio Zamora. *My white boy sadness.*

As a folklorist, someone who's spent his whole adult life
studying the planet's cultures, I've developed a long list of inspi-
rational quotes, optimistic catchphrases, wise words.

"Six feet of earth make all men of one size," says an old
American proverb.

James Russell Lowell, speaking of President Garfield, said,
"The soil out of which such men as he are made is good to be
born on . . . to die for and be buried in."

But no soothing thoughts came to me that day on the freeway.
Instead, it was Dickens I recalled. Simple, brutal, direct: "Old
Marley was dead as a doornail."

At first, among the tow trucks, flashing lights, and emergency
personnel, I couldn't see my parents or my wife. By the time

I understood what was happening, the ambulance attendants (brown coats, muted, efficient expressions) had laid sheets across their bodies. Their contours looked massive. Surely that wasn't my father under there. Surely not Jean. Such lumpy *weight*. No. They were light. Graceful. Swift. Their laughter was lovely, their hop-skips silly and free whenever they felt happy.

The owner of the truck, an independent yardman, had also died in the crash. No family. Uninsured.

I'd been behind the wheel. My father's car. Driving us to a new seafood restaurant in Galveston.

All his life, Dad had ridden around in behemoths—Oldsmobiles and Cadillacs, impervious to impact. But in 1987 a negligence suit from an injured employee had wiped out his refinery company and most of his savings. (The inheritance I'd always been promised was suddenly gone on the wind.) In his forced retirement he'd bought a Honda hatchback.

I was the only one wearing a seatbelt: the reason I walked away that night, a vague, bald official told me later. He assured me I'd done everything possible to avoid the accident. No way to brake in time. A bear of a cop, a kid, patted my arm. "It was just," he said, "one of those things, eh?"

For months afterward I stayed busy, quiet, letting other people talk, interviewing the Thuots and the Zamoras. Their stories got me through those first awful weeks. *Tell me more about the mountains. What's Jalisco like in the summer?*

In our five years together, Jean and I had joked about aging and dying but, like most people, we thought we'd live forever.

My parents' wills didn't specify where or how they wanted to be buried. I'd never heard them talk about it.

I don't recall, in the fog of last year, how I finally made up my mind. I *do* remember worrying that if I waited too long to act, they'd all mummify, like Norman Bates's old lady in *Psycho*. That happened in Houston despite the humidity. Occasionally, a story made the paper: a cop, alerted to the smell, would find the preserved body of an elderly man or woman in a rocking chair, in a warm, dry house the neighbors never checked.

Also, of course, I knew the folk legends: Saint Francis Xavier had been saved intact since the sixteenth century in the town of Goa on the Indian subcontinent. Supplicants were no longer allowed to see his corpse; a worshipper bit off his toe one year in a fever of religious ecstasy.

Clearly, embroiled in such thoughts, I was not in my right mind when I had to inter my family.

I settled on the Magnolia Blossom Cemetery on South Ruthven Street, a pretty little place I'd passed many times on my way to work. Predominantly Mexican Catholic, it contains some of the best *grutas*, or personal shrines, in Texas. Sandstone, reddish-brown lava. All of its graves face east: sunrise, the day's fresh hope.

5.

Tonight as I pull into the parking garage, the newspaper building blazes blue and orange under the freeway's sodium lights. The garage smells of oil and old rotting lunch meats stuffed into dumpsters (left over from Sam's Kosher Deli nearby).

"Evening, Bob," I greet the security guard.

He hitches his belt up over his belly. His keys rattle. "Hiya, Mr. Palmer." He's lethargic and slow, with the patchy red face of a drinker. Probably he'd be useless in an emergency but his presence reassures me. He's one of the city's familiar signposts, someone whose location I can always count on.

I take the elevator to the fifth floor where I type-and-enter my days. As soon as my father lost his savings (he'd been the primary benefactor of my fledgling little press) I found this job at the paper, penning obituaries and occasional fillers. I had to adjust quickly to being poor, or at least poorer than I'd ever been.

"Nothing fancy, now. Don't try to be goddam Balzac," the managing editor, a pugnacious old gent named Penrose, told me the morning he took me on. "These days—last time I checked the gloomy goddam figures—the public's reading capacity hovers somewhere between second and third grade. You want to be literary, go park yourself on a street corner, shouting lousy poems about the lousy goddam . . . whatever."

"What about news?" I asked. "Generating my own stories?"

"Forget about news. I hand you a simple format, you fill it in. Got it?"

"Got it," I said.

Most of my colleagues at the paper are quick and efficient, in and out of the office each day with barely a grumble or flourish, but a small group of us—Tony Lyons, from the church beat (the most profane man I've ever met), Ed Branigan, a typesetter, Scott Lehman, who covers the cops, and me—we meet late nightly for cards. None of us have family waiting at home. Tony's separated from his wife. Ed and Scott are both divorced. We're all insomniacs—which is what you say when you're grown instead of admitting you're afraid of the dark.

When I bustle in tonight the boys are dealing their third round on Tony's metal desk. Cigarette smoke swarms the snicking yellow lights. The radio's tuned to the blues: *My man's a busted tire on a muddy old road . . .*

"George, man, am I glad to see you," Tony says. "This game sucks with three people."

"Just like love."

"You in?"

"I'm in." I stow my recordings of Julio and Mr. Thuot in my gray steel desk.

"Tony, man, you *shuffle* these cards?" Ed asks.

"He never shuffles the cards," Scott says. "Watch him. He just messes them up a little."

I pull up a chair.

"'Shuffle' is not in his vocabulary. 'Shuffle' is a sacred, ancient wisdom he's somehow failed to grasp."

"Been yakking with your fuckin' rice-eaters?" Tony says to me.

I used to snap at him when he'd talk this way but it never shut him up. Now I count silently to ten and let it go.

He runs a hand across his bald spot, which is shaped a little like Australia. "See you and raise you," he says to Ed.

"Cold, brother."

"Call."

"Boat."

"Damn. You *didn't* shuffle." Ed grabs his paunch as though he's had a pain.

Tony reels off a series of golfing jokes, each involving a Protestant minister, a rabbi and a priest. They all end with some form of indecent exposure.

Scott and Ed are clawing into their wallets now, inflicting on each other the latest snapshots of their kids. They tamp back tears.

I don't know what I'd do without these guys. But tonight—in fact, for quite some time—I don't know why I hang with them, either.

"You're drifting, George," Tony warns me. "Cut 'em."

I tap the deck. "They're good."

Scott's pale and thin from eating mostly Oreos. He plucks the cookies apart and chucks the creamy side—his nod to good health, he says. Ed's a sure-fire heart attack: tomorrow, the day after. You can almost hear him ticking.

And here I am. Pathetic.

"How many?"

"What?"

"Cards, George. How many cards?"

"Oh. Two."

"I know all about you," Scott said to me one day. We were standing near the men's room with its river-water smell and its big red door. Scott is short and aggressive. He never finished his psychology degree in college and clearly he regrets it. Around the poker table he claims he can read our faces, catch our bluffs. But he always winds up losing.

"What is it you think you know about me, Scott?"

He swallowed the last of the ham sandwich he'd been nibbling along with his cookies and crumpled his yellow napkin. "The reason you're so quiet. Why you like just listening to others. Taping them and stuff."

"And why is that?"

"Your accident." He can't hide his pride whenever he drops these little insight-bombs on his buddies. He's lucky we still let him play with us. "You think you should have died, right?"

Pressed against the bathroom door, I felt like a well-thumbed poster for a long-past event. "Scott, listen—"

"Survivor guilt. Why me?" He wrapped his fingers in his napkin and poked me in the chest. "Naturally, it troubles you. So you imagine yourself gone."

"You're full of shit."

He grinned.

Tonight, as the fellows joke and laugh—Scott watching me gleefully, anticipating my every bluff—I fold and fold and fold.

***

Driving home, late, I smell the city's labors: dirt and sweat, the soft tar of the roads, the balanced tension of girders, rust and air. Lights pulse. Jean loved nights like this, stark and steamy.

Magnolia trees cluster around paint-peeled wooden houses on the edge of the First Ward. Moonlight glints off the glass of the downtown towers, panes blue and brown, green and gold. As the moon rises higher, it makes glowing whips of phone lines webbed above hot streets.

The no-zoned neighborhoods make Houston a constant surprise: a palm reader sits next to a Republican campaign head-quarters, a hot tub dealer next to a strict-bricked Baptist church. One minute the city's a wise old matriarch, calm, cheerful, cautious. Next thing you know, she's ripped off her mask to reveal a snide, sneaky kid.

Tonight, my part of town—run-down, poor, slammed hard by AIDS—is dark and quiet. If I'd had the money I might've moved after Jean died. But I still live in the cheap little house we shared at the end, a two-bedroom, musty with dust and too many memories. It's in the old Montrose neighborhood, behind a small outfit, Sno King, that manufactures ice-makers. Sometimes, deep in the night, an out-of-whack ice-maker flings watery cubes at the plant's walls. Lying in bed together, Jean and I used to laugh about the sounds.

Or we'd argue about having kids, after making love.

I see now how much I tormented her, always mentioning Monica and Kate. Or Manuel. "He's so pretty, Jean, and lively," I told her the night I met the Zamoras. I played her a tape of his voice.

"George, *please!*"

She told me once that I was a "professional fuck-up." "I don't think people want to read your stuff, do they?"

But when we first got together she said she loved me for my "empathy skills": "Sometimes they're buried a little deep, but they're there." The first night I spent at her place I offered to draw her a bath. She sat on her bed and cried. "No one's ever done that for me before," she said. "It's so sweet." She reached for my hand. I dried her face with a towel. "In spite of your rough surface, you're a caretaker, aren't you?"

I'd never thought of myself that way but I liked who I was in her eyes. She gave me stability, maturity, calm. As folks tend to say in pigskin-crazy Texas, we made a pretty good team.

Now each ice-ping conjures her lovely face.

"Tony was the big winner tonight," I tell her. Gauzy as frost, she's wafting in front of my pillow. Every night she visits me like this. She's wearing a pale-white dress and blouse. Perfect hair. "I dropped forty bucks."

She circles my head. I curse my imagination. With a punch of my pillow (aiming straight for its cottony heart) Jean disappears, only to be replaced by the vibrant spirits of my current life: Mrs. Thuot sipping tea, Manuel shouting in the street, Lira hiding a puffy red welt on her face . . .

Fuck.

I shut my eyes and concentrate on my breathing.

Two years ago—three?—Jean planted a skinny apple tree in our front yard. Now it whispers in a flat southerly breeze: *Shhh. Shhh.*

6.

On Saturdays and Sundays I hate to impose myself on the Thuots and the Zamoras. After looking for work all week, scrambling for food, they've earned a rest from the great white world.

So I drive over to the Shamrock Six, the multiplex I used to spend my days in whenever Jean was teaching and Kelly and the girls were busy at the Casa. It's the most Southern place in town, like a holy-roller country church. "Yeah! You got it, Slick!" the audience screams at actors moving stiffly toward a shoot-out or a teary embrace. Generations merge here at the Early-Bird Show to confirm their fellowship, their superiority to the fools onscreen.

"Brother *dead!*"

"No he ain't. He gonna rip that sucker's drawers."

"*Fine*-lookin' mama!"

Meanwhile, the rest of Houston, belonging to the wide-open West, whips about in its cars—one person, two at the most, per set of wheels—pursuing happiness, Manifest Destiny, today's equivalent of gold: a makeover, a microwave oven, a seat behind home plate.

Today, *Blood Orgy* is showing at the Shamrock and I'm mighty content with my popcorn and my spot in the back row with its wide-angle view of the theater and the families laughing, quibbling, jostling for a peek at the screen. An old woman wipes a baby's face. Two boys wrestle over a Milky Way bar. A middle-aged couple sneaks a kiss. Then we're drenched in humming blue light and an actress seems to be swallowed by an alien werewolf or a radioactive schnauzer—I can't tell.

I sit through two showings.

Outside, as I'm leaving after four and half hours in the dark, I see a big, oak-colored man beneath the marquee grab a woman's chin. "You *look* at me when I'm talking to you!" he says. "That compute wit you, bitch?" They're standing in a crowd of sweaty kids. When he drops his hand, the woman closes her eyes and rubs her face.

I blink, trying to adjust my vision to the light.

I think of Lira Zamora. For months, I've given myself sorry excuses: *too messy, none of my business, troubles of my own . . .*

In the presence of actual violence I realize how flimsy my little evasions are. I've been an asshole. For months and months. Doing nothing. Dreaming of jackpots. Talking to ghosts.

Move! I think, watching the man shove the woman forward into the parking lot. But I simply stand and watch. His hand makes a fat clamp on her arm. The sun feels cold on my head.

* * *

Monday evening, I swing by the Zamoras' at seven just as I figure Lira is stepping off the bus. Julio's still got half an hour at the take-out.

I've brought a couple new Spidermans for Manuel and a copy of *Job Opportunities: Houston and Environs* for Lira. Cal let me have it at half-price. It's a year out of date.

Lira is not happy to see me. As she walks from the bus at the corner Manuel runs past me on the porch. "You can't catch me, Superman!" he shouts. "I've got *Kryptonite* in my *shorts!*"

I take a play-swipe at him then fall to my knees. "Oh no! I'm losing my strength!" I say.

"Ha ha! The world is mine!" He rushes into the house.

"Hello," I say softly to Lira, standing and brushing dust from my pants. "Can I help you with those?"

She frowns and tightens her grip on three small grocery bags. "No thank you." She's got Frida Kahlo eyebrows: black and wiry, a single little rope.

"I've been meaning to bring you a copy of this." I wave the job book at her.

In fact, I'd spent the rest of my weekend planning my visit, practicing what I might say to her. I remembered it hadn't gone well the first time I'd tried to catch her alone. Who did I think I was? Her rescuer? Her hero? Spiderman, for chrissakes?

"Very kind," she says. She's gathered her hair into a bun the size of a tennis ball.

On her cheek, a dark green bruise, big as an oak leaf.

"The kids? They're okay?" I say.

"Yes. Fine," she says. In her pink-and-yellow dress she's not much bigger than a child herself.

I reach to touch the swelling on her face. She startles. I pull back. My fingers haven't felt a woman's skin since Jean. "I'm sorry, Lira. It's none of my business. But I've been worried about you. I've been wanting to talk to you for a while, but—" I'm aware that my words are too intimate. I don't know her well enough to say these things. "Can you tell me?"

She moves past me into the house.

"Has someone been hitting you?" I ask, standing in the doorway. Suddenly, I feel a ghostly sting on *my* cheek.

"No. No one," she answers.

"Julio?"

"You're very thoughtful, but—"

"Lira, I'd like to be your friend."

She sets her bags on the coffee table. The kids run and scream in a back room. "Quiet!" she yells. Then to me: "Julio is happy to tell you his stories. But I never agreed to this."

It's true. A year or so ago, I came poking into this neighborhood, risking ridicule, indifference, even violence, looking for people who would talk to me. Most folks turned away. Julio, gregarious, generous, surprised me by welcoming me into his home.

Lira had never been friendly.

"I don't mean to impose." I step into the house. "But . . . well, the thing is, I've come to care for your family."

"What about your own family?" she says. "Don't they need you?"

I can't answer her. Not yet. My cheek burns.

"Quiet!" she screams again at her kids, stopping a heavy thumping in the back room. "You want to hear a story, is that it?" she asks me.

"Yes. Sure."

She looks at me, looks at her feet. "All right. All right then." Some kind of moisture leaks from one of the grocery bags. Flies batter the front screen door. She loosens her bun. She grips her hair as if she's clinging to the rigging of a ship. "When I was a girl in Jalisco, my mother sent me each day to buy eggs from a neighbor who lived across the highway from our house," she begins. "It was a very busy highway, leading to big market centers far away to the west. Buses and trucks, much noise, keeping us all awake, my brothers and sisters, even at night. Whenever she sent me for the eggs, my mother warned me so hard to be careful—she wanted to impress on me the danger—I always cried, carrying my little basket."

Dogs bark down the block. I'm wishing I'd jammed my Sony into my pocket but it's still in the car. Cicadas creak in the trees.

"One day, I was on my way home—proud of the six or seven large brown eggs I'd chosen—when I saw an old woman, a flower-seller clutching dozens of white roses, slowly crossing the road ahead of me. I glanced down the highway. I heard the rumble of a truck, the shifting of its gears, awful, like a cat's whine . . . the woman shuffled toward the center of the road . . . can you guess the rest of my story?"

The sun is setting behind Houston's huge glass buildings, nearby. The house is getting dark. "I'm afraid I can."

"I shouted and shouted. Perhaps she was deaf. I'll never forget her skirts, beautiful black and red, whipping in the wind of the truck. The scattered flowers and the scream. I fell to the dirt. Dropped my basket. All the eggs cracked."

She stands for a moment watching light fade through her lace curtains. "I don't even have words in my own language to describe how this memory makes me feel . . . how it twists me inside . . . and so, telling stories to *you*, in English—"

"You just did a bang-up job," I say.

She shakes her head.

"Believe it or not, I understand what you feel, Lira. Really." I hesitate. "I lost my family. Last year. On a highway."

She searches my face. I don't know what she sees but she softens a little.

Just then Manuel lurches, giggling, into the room, bumping my legs. He clamps his mother's calf. "Mama, I'm hungry!"

In a mad race the other kids swarm her: Angelina, Roberto, Maria. Chatito, the youngest, cries from his crib in the back of the house.

Lira gives me a weary smile. "Maybe you should join us next month for the Day of the Dead," she says. "When people we love leave this world of sorrows, we prepare their favorite dishes for them. You know the custom?"

"Yes. A sort of communion with family spirits?"

"And with those of us who must go on."

"Hungry hungry hungry!" Manuel yelps.

I offer to watch the babies while Lira fixes supper. When I turn to pick up Roberto, I see Julio slouched motionless in the doorway. He's holding a white apron stained with hot mustard, sweet-and-sour sauce. He's sweating and tired. "George," he says glumly.

"Julio."

"What are *you* doing here?"

"I dropped by. Just to see how things were going."

"Lira didn't tell me you were coming."

She shivers and rubs her arms. "I didn't know," she says. Shadows drape the room. "Excuse me." She heads for the kitchen. The kids scramble after her, a noisy gaggle.

Julio stares at me strangely. I've never seen him so quiet. Have I broken a rule, entering his house, meeting his wife while he was away?

Then, as swiftly as a tornado switching directions, he offers me a smile. "You got the transcript?"

"The what?"

"The last interview we did." He shuffles into the pantry next to the kitchen.

I confess, "I haven't typed it up."

He squeezes his apron and tosses it into the washer. From the dryer he pulls a wad of laundry, still soggy. "Why not? You know I love reading about my family."

"Julio, the fact is, the press is in arrears."

"Rears?" He kicks the machine.

"I told you I'm running out of money. I can barely make my rent right now. The books don't sell—"

"This fucker. We didn't hook it up right."

"The chain stores won't touch them. The guy at Cal's—he's the only one who's shown any real interest in the past, and even *he* won't take them anymore. To tell you the truth, I'm wondering if there's any point in writing a new one."

"Fuckin' *Jamón*," Julio says.

Does he mean *me*? Yes, he's staring at me. The storm has shifted again.

A can opener buzzes in the kitchen.

Julio shoves a shirt and pants into the dryer. "So. I gave you all that information for nothing?"

"No. Of course not."

He's tapping his feet rapidly: big, bare, brown on the gritty yellow carpet.

I move away from him. Surely it's the dryer that's got him upset. The long day at work. "I'm looking for new funding," I say. A lie. No one'll back me with no hope of profit. "I'll let you know."

"To you it's just a *project*, George. But it's *my goddam life*." He slaps his chest.

I hear an eerie echo of my wife: "It's *my body*," she told me once, early in our marriage, when we talked about having kids. "One little spurt and the story's over for you, George, but me—assuming my plumbing still works—I'll swell up big as a house. No thanks."

"It's okay," I tell Julio now.

"No one cares about *my* life, right? I'll die invisible. Just like all the other wetbacks."

"Julio, man—"

"I have to clean this apron now, George. Excuse me."

"Your stories *are* important to me. All right?"

He balls his fists and slams the top of the dryer. "Why am *I* the only one carrying his goddam weight around here? The only one keeping his word?"

Lira drops a glass in the kitchen.

Julio's shoulders sag. "*Hijo!*" he yells out a dusty pantry window. Roberto has just scampered by with a ball. "Get your little ass in here and pick up your room! I can't do it all!"

Julio turns a round plastic dial on the dryer. It lurches against the wall.

Quietly, I let myself out. In the front doorway, I turn and catch Lira's eye. She's somber, sadly pretty. Her body droops. *I never agreed to this.*

7.

In the mirror of the men's room at work I examine my face. Nothing. My cheek still stings.

In the newsroom the guys are talking about bringing new blood into the game. "Who could we get?" Scott says.

I tell them about Cal. I know he's a player.

"Hey, if his money's good and his card savvy's poor, I have no objection," Ed says. "I mean, the man owns a bookstore. How savvy can he be, right?"

I shuffle the deck. Nine of hearts, three of spades, queen, queen. I'm imagining things: both queens resemble Jean.

There it is again. A throb in my cheek.

"Hit me with a big one," Scott says.

"Two for me."

"One."

"George, you in this next round?"

"No. Deal past me." I stand and slouch against the water cooler. Bubbles blast through the bottle, a tiny depth-charge. I rub my face.

"Dirty mama," a singer sings on the radio.

You want to hear a story, is that it?

My chest heaves. What is happening to me? I think.

Bruises.

A shifting of gears on the highway.

The day of the crash.

I don't remember if she'd discovered one of Kelly's old letters—though Kelly and I were finished by then—or if I'd been stupid enough to mention kids again. But Jean and I fought.

Later, behind the wheel of my father's car, I still felt her slap on my cheek. "You didn't have time to breathe, man, much less brake or change course," an investigator told me afterward. But I swear I recall a second or two, an instant of instinct, just before the pickup swerved into my lane, when I took my eyes off the road and met my wife's chilly stare in the rear-view.

Tony slams the deck in front of my empty chair. "Get over here, George, and cut 'em. Okay. Low spade in the hole splits the pot. Ante up, boys."

Scott watches me closely across the table. He chomps half an Oreo. "You shouldn't be here, George," he says. "Not if you're not going to concentrate."

"Hey, I'm a survivor," I say. "What about you?" And I cough up the last bit of scratch from my pocket.

***

In the dark I listen to Sno King rattle. Beneath the sharp thwacks, the rustling of apple leaves outside my bedroom window. The day Jean planted the tree she told me, "When I was little my mother used to read me bedtime stories. Nothing thrilled me more than the tales of Johnny Appleseed. It was the most wonderful thing, imagining this happy fellow spreading this lovely fruit around the world. I begged her and begged her for an apple tree in our yard. Finally, my father bought one and for years I watched it grow."

I rubbed her back. She was sore from shoveling dirt.

"Then in college, studying physics—Newton's apple, right? I was delighted all over again. Gravity, spreading seeds . . . for me, apples became, I don't know, some kind of solid connection to the earth. I guess it sounds silly. But I swore I'd plant an apple tree wherever I lived."

"It's not silly," I said. I drew a bath for her and washed the dirt from her arms.

Now she's listing in the bedroom's warm air, about three feet from my face. Diffuse as lamplight, she wears the cotton gloves she wore to plant the tree. A faint odor of loam.

She removes one of the gloves and gently rubs the side of my face.

"Thank you," I say. She smiles, shimmers like water, then fades.

***

In the middle of the night I wake from my first wet dream in—how many years? Since long before my marriage. I was walking along the bayou with Lira, the water like silk. I reached to touch a bruise on her face. She opened her mouth and took my thumb between her lips.

I felt the warmth at my waist.

Now the rain comes hard, stirring mud in the beds where Jean used to grow marigolds, roses, lilies, thyme and dill. The apple tree moves to and fro, making a sound like someone clapping.

8.

"Heads up, boyo! We need a pair of first class obits here," Penrose announced this morning. "They have to be somber and respectful, mindful of the city's major loss." He handed me a packet of photos. A personal injury lawyer and a real estate developer, dead of a heart attack and a stroke, respectively.

"What? No 'Good riddance'?" I said. "'O happy day'?"

"Save that searing wit for your two-bit card games, son. And on that other matter—it's good research. But no one wants to read about it."

He'd agreed to look at *Houston's Latin Refugees* when I took a chance and mentioned it to him one day, suggesting he could run sections of it in the paper, a two- or three-part series, maybe. Community service.

"It's a downer. People want to feel good about their town."

Yes, and what tourists always take to be charm is a manifestation of economic deprivation for the locals, I thought. "Okay. Thanks for considering it."

On my lunch break, I offer to run by Sam's Deli. Ed wants turkey, Tony a hoagie. Ash smudges the air from an aggravated volcano south of the Rio Grande. In front of me, a flatbed pickup hauls empty Cokes. The bottles fill with powder.

I make a quick stop at Cal's. The Bookmobile is parked by his curb. A year ago, before falling oil prices pinched his sales, he'd bought this custom-made van as an advertising gimmick. Plexiglas, solid, tinted brown. A see-through floorboard. Every time a customer spent a hundred dollars or more, Cal would give them a ride in the Bookmobile. "Cruising the freeways with only a river of sweet air between you and freedom and the road," he'd say. For a while it was a popular sales ploy. Now he's into raffles.

"Thought you'd sold that clunker," I say, walking in. "I haven't seen it in months."

He's stacking ratty paperbacks: cookbooks, astrology guides, an unauthorized biography of Mamie Eisenhower. "Ray's learning to drive so I been lending him my horsepower," he says. "Boy's a damn Formula One fireball when he scoots behind the wheel."

"How's his dad?"

"Goner. Ghost."

"Jesus, Cal. I'm sorry."

Ray emerges from a tiny bathroom in the back. "Mr. Palmer! Good to see you," he says.

"Hey Ray. You too." He's clean-shaven now. "I hear you're about ready to hit the road. Got your car picked out? Classic Mustang? Thunderbird?"

He grins and lowers his head. "Haven't had much time to look lately. My dad, you know."

"Sure."

"Excuse me," he says, wiping his nose. He scuffles back to the john.

"Poor kid," I say.

"Yeah. Billy's a damn fighter but it looks like this is one ol' bear he's not going to beat."

"Can I help?"

He tosses Mamie onto *The True Story of Jackie O*. "Tell me again about your game."

I'd mentioned our poker nights to him and he said he'd think about it. He hadn't played cards since his brother got sick and he was feeling a little rusty: "I'm afraid I'll show up and not look like I know what I'm doing."

"They're a friendly bunch," I tell him now.

Ray's back, trying to smile.

Cal slaps a discount tag on M.F.K. Fisher. "I don't want to be razzed by a load of assholes. I don't need that in my life."

"They're not like that. Really." Well. Just a little.

"Maybe you two could work a deal, Unc. You stock some of Mr. Palmer's books, he puts in a good word for you with his pals," Ray says.

I want to kiss the kid.

Delivery trucks scurry past us on the street. Pizzas, furniture, meat. Bless our culture of exchange.

Cal rubs his face. "When's your next game?"

"I'll let you know when I drop the books off."

He shakes his head but he's grinning.

I tell Ray I'd be happy to give him a driving lesson some night.

"I'd like that," he says.

"Save your card money, George," Cal says. "You're going to need a barrelful."

***

"*Turkey*, George. I ordered turkey," Ed says, pulling apart his sandwich. "This is—what the hell is it? Aluminum siding?"

On my desk a scribbled message: "Call Julio Zamora—Urgent."

A woman speaking rapid Spanish answers the phone.

"I'm sorry, I can't . . . can you please slow down?" I say.

Impatiently, she says, "Mr. Zamora cannot talk to anyone right now."

"*Que pasó?*"

In stilted English the woman explains to me that Mrs. Zamora came home from the employment agency late this morning and, without a word to her husband, picked up her babies and tossed them into Buffalo Bayou.

"Tossed?" I say. "What do you mean, 'tossed'?"

"Like dolls, sir. Like old newspapers."

"Was anyone hurt?"

Chatito, ten weeks old, drowned, she says. Roberto is missing. Manuel and the others are in shock. The police had handcuffed Mrs. Zamora and driven her away.

"What's up, man?" Tony watches me from his desk. "Trouble in taco land?"

Count to ten. "Any calls for me, take a message, okay?" I tell him.

"Hey George," Ed calls. "You going out again? Can you bring me back some turkey?"

At the mouth of the garage, pulling out in my car, I wave at Bob, half-asleep in his concrete security booth. He doesn't look up. I speed down Main Street past Indonesian restaurants and a Pizza Inn. Car exhaust hangs in willows along the median. The Astrodome rises like an old, pallid whale to the south.

Julio's neighbors are talking in tight circles on their lawns: men with long shirt-tails sipping canned beer. Children play near the curb. On the horizon, at the end of the street, Houston's glassed-in banks tower together like massive slats in a cyclone fence. The bayou boils around fallen oak limbs curled like big arthritic hands. Five or six cops unroll a strip of yellow tape among low bushes. "Back. Get back, please." "No floater here," one man shouts into a walkie-talkie. "Water's moving pretty fast. We're gonna need boats and divers downstream."

Julio's slumped on his gray-checkered couch, drunk and in tears. Behind him, two whispering young policemen. I tell them I'm a friend. They check my driver's license, call in my name. Finally, they let me sit down.

"Julio." I touch his arm. His shirt is limp with sweat. "Julio, what happened?"

Bleary face. "*No se . . .* "

"Is Lira all right?"

"I don't know. I don't know, George."

"Was she angry? Upset about something? How could—"

"*I don't know*! She was worn out. The bus. The kids." He spreads his hands. "What could I have done?"

"It's all right. Take your time."

Sunlight bastes the room through the open door.

Julio lowers his voice. I lean close to him. "For a while this morning, after she came home, I wanted to sleep with her, you know. But she said no, that was the problem. We couldn't afford more kids. I guess . . . I guess I got mad and . . . " He kicks the table in front of us. I jump. The cops turn to look, still whispering. "Then she grabbed Chatito and went out the door with him. Clutching a rosary in her hand. I didn't know what was happening. When she came back without him and picked up Angelina, I knew something was wrong, but she was so *strong*, man. I couldn't believe the power in her arms. I'd had too many beers."

I notice a tiny wooden crucifix on the wall above the television, a Black Christ nailed to its arms. I haven't seen it before. I ask Julio about it. As the Day of the Dead approached, Lira had become more and more "religious," he says—by which he means "sullen and withdrawn."

On the television set, next to a fat candle, I see four tiny clay tablets. Tierras del Santos: pieces of earth, each stamped with a saint's grave face. I knew that among certain Latin peoples these cakes are eaten or dissolved in water as a drink to ease menstrual pain.

Jesus. "Julio? Julio, is Lira pregnant again?"

He stares at me.

"It's none of my business, man. But you know . . . there are ways to prevent that."

"We watch the moon. Lira always says—" He shakes his head.

"And the other kids?"

"The man in the ambulance thinks they'll be okay."

"Roberto?"

"*No se.*" He grips my hand. "I don't know what happened, George. We were a happy family. Lira loved Chatito. She was a good mother to those babies."

A ripped Spiderman comic lies at our feet, beneath the wobbly table. I glance at the cops. "Julio, have they checked your immigration status?"

"I'm not sure."

"If they ask you about it, don't tell them anything. You're entitled to a lawyer. Do you understand?"

"Yes."

"Mr. Zamora?" One of the policemen asks Julio to follow him onto the porch.

"You have my work number, right?" I say. "If there's anything I can do, let me know. Julio?"

"Okay," he says.

I squeeze his arm.

"George?"

"Yes?"

"Tell them."

"Sure. Anything."

"Tell them our story."

9.

Air-conditioners hum in the city. The freeway shakes. Through my car speakers Lightnin' Hopkins croaks:

> You know, I drink wine for this reason
> And this is the reason why
> It give me a good feelin' in the mornin'
> It make me feel like tellin' real good—
> I ain't talk'm bout a lie
> But you *know* . . .

He strokes the strings like a drum, beats them hard with his hand, up down up down, I turn the tape player up, *that's right*, and then you're down some more son better watch your updown and then you're turned around.

Swirls of ash gather from the Mexican volcano. This wild-assed city of ours: it's too fucking much.

No sane person could raise a family here. Pure Death. On the freeway. In dirty, roiling water. Ashes, fights and slaps.

Through my open window I take it all in: a muffler the size of a boat *my baby she left me this mornin'* a thirty-foot roach ("24-hour exterminators") kidney-shaped swimming pool propped on a pole. Captain Kirk and Mr. Spock ("Join the Voyage at 6!") "Pregnant? Emergency Call . . . " burgers and doughnuts and dogs and *maybe she doin' me wrong say yes she doin' me wrong say baby*

I been acryin' I been drunker'n a skunk since June. Eyebrows and rheumatism, arthritis and armadillos, low-tar smokes, *The Wall Street Journal say yes she is say baby* "Let's All Be There!" Sugar's and Spinners and Cooters. Fizz, Biff's, Bill's. Tires thrumming on the concrete. Dependency City: Alcoholism? Child abuse? Drugs? Want to Talk? Any Time of Night Just Pick Up A . . .

Quick exit onto Montrose.

A radio tune tumbles out of an open apartment window. A teenage girl carrying a slim gold purse, wearing red high heels, strolls the edge of a park.

My, my, my.

Southern folk wisdom says a man whose drink is laced with a lady's menstrual blood will always be her slave.

She waves at me. I zip through the light. A McDonald's wrapper kicks up over my hood and dithers away down the street.

I slow then circle back toward Main.

No matter what, for me, there's no getting out of this place. Even if it *is* too fucking much. I've buried my family here. My keepsakes. My history.

And why leave, anyway? Life's brimming here in the big, bad Bayou City.

***

Much later—after work, after cards, after losing a stack of ten-dollar bills (our final game before Cal joins the group)—I end up at the Shamrock. The Midnight Show.

Danger, Incorporated. Black gangsters waging an LA coke war.

"*Fly* threads, brother!"

"Make that sucker eat it!"

"Motherfucker's *toast*!"

The crowd is cheerful and warm. I scan the seats, looking for the woman I saw last time, wondering if she's surviving.

Then the lights are up, smoky, spooky blue. Folks are filing out.

"Wake up, white boy!" someone sings at me. "Yoo-hoo." Laughter. "Say, man. Party just startin'!"

10.

Through late-season leaves on the bayou's banks I watch police boats putt around puckered brown whirlpools. They're searching for Roberto. Young men in wetsuits slog through shallows and mud. Onlookers come and go, eating bag lunches, reading paperbacks and newspapers, gossiping.

I follow the bend for about two miles, past a ruined campsite for street people. The cops busted it up earlier this month. For nearly six years laid-off oil workers pitched tents or tarps here or slept in blown-gasket cars. Their neighbors, poor families like the Thuots and the Zamoras living in run-down rental homes, didn't complain but folks in outlying areas did. "It's a transient population, drug-addicted and mentally *off*," said a woman who lived a mile away. "They break into houses like mine, looking for pawnable items."

I wrote several obits of men from the camp who'd died during winter freezes or whose bodies had been found in the bayou. At one point, Penrose (who didn't really seem to understand what was happening there) thought there might be an interesting story or two at the camp. He asked me to look into it. Naturally, he didn't like what I brought him. "There's not *one* positive angle here," he said. "If we had a case of someone pulling himself out of poverty, finding a job . . . "

Now all that's left of the place is scorched grass from old cooking fires.

The river is placid here, near where the Thuots get their bath water. Two Black boys straddle pine logs on the bank, pitching fishing lines into the current. "Catch anything?" I ask, stepping through brambles.

"Naw. Ain't nothing worth catching," says one of the boys. His companion spits into the water.

Farther down, ivy snags my feet. It's not just the camp: about three-quarters of the obits I write are for folks who drown in the stream.

"Police divers Monday recovered the bodies of two men whose Toyota truck collided with a car on the Eastex Freeway and plummeted sixty feet into Buffalo Bayou. The southbound lanes of the freeway were closed for twelve hours."

"Police authorities surmise that an arm discovered in the bayou near the Jensen Street Bridge belongs to a man seen yesterday clinging to an oak limb in a torrent following flash flooding this weekend."

One beautiful spring afternoon last year, a mounted police officer's horse—a ten-year-old gelding named Einstein—got spooked, apparently by a discarded tangle of bright orange mesh in the grass. The horse slipped into the water and sank beneath the Capitol Street Bridge. An hour later, its body surfaced and workers removed it using a heavy-duty dump truck.

The city's most infamous drowning occurred twenty years ago. Cops beat Joe Campos Torres so badly on the street, the booking sergeant refused to accept him into any city jail. The officers dragged Torres to a site near the bayou and whaled on him some more. Then he either jumped or was pushed into the water. None of the cops involved in the incident spent more than a year in prison.

I could recite these details all day and they wouldn't take my mind off Lira or help me place her behavior in any kind of graspable context.

I try my trusty folklore but it doesn't help much either. What does local history say? The bayou was named for the buffalo gar seen navigating its waters. But I've collected other anecdotes suggesting that eighteenth-century Spanish explorers called it "Arroyo de Cibilo" or "Ditch of Bison" on their earliest maps. Apparently, the explorers witnessed Native Americans driving mammoths over the silted banks to cripple them and make them easy targets for their spears.

There's supposed to be a Confederate schooner in the water here somewhere. I've got recorded testimony from an ex-slave's son who claims to have danced on the ship's ruined deck during a severe drought in the summer of 1908.

I emerge from the underbrush, amazed at the amount of detritus in my head.

"Water Under the Bridge: Exotic Seafood since 1947" says a metal sign on a dark green building near the bank. "Drum, sheepshead, croaker, Mahi from Hawaii."

Through a window in the building I see the shadow of a man moving among jars of tentacles in clear, pickled brine, among fishing nets filled with crusty clam shells, swaying from the ceiling. I smell lemon and oysters.

Another man steps out back wearing a slick rubber apron spattered with pink and yellow fish guts. He's wiping his hands on a newspaper.

Through bent willow trees trailing the tips of their limbs in the water, sketching thin, dirty ripples in tiny concentric rings come the muted spasms of boat motors circling, circling, circling upstream.

11.

Three days. No word from Julio. His house appears to be empty. No one answers the phone.

I've asked Scott, whose beat it is, to learn what he can from the cops, which isn't much: Lira has been arraigned on capital murder charges. "A recent law in Texas makes multiple killings a capital offense," Scott explained to me. "Tough luck for your friend. This assumes that the other kid—Roberto?—is dead." For now, her location is a well-guarded secret. Her Mexican citizenship complicates the paperwork so the DA's office wants to keep her under wraps. "All I can tell you is she's not in the Criminal Courts Building. I've checked the new facility over on San Jacinto and Baker Streets. They don't call it a jail. They call it an 'Adult Detention Zone,'" Scott said. "But for all its high-tech gadgetry it's still the same old bars and walls. Anyway, the pugs who run the place won't talk to me."

"Thanks for trying."

"No problem." He studied me. "People just keep vanishing on you, don't they?"

"Not the *right* people," I said.

* * *

At Prince's Drive-In, a teenage girl grilling burgers tells me Julio's apron has been "hanging from that meathook in the kitchen since Sat'day, late, when the son-of-a-bitch was s'pose to show up to relieve my draggin' ass." Her braces flash in reflected light from grease burbling in the fryer. "Ain't seen hide nor hair of him."

At the Chinese take-out, the assistant manager, a young Taiwanese, shrugs when I mention Julio. Six or seven women, Black and Asian, sit at a table in the kitchen peeling shrimp. They sweep the shells onto scattered newspapers on the floor.

"Lavonda say she gettin' the house *and* the car," says one. She's tall with short hair in tangled sprouts. She tosses wedges of orange meat into a pot boiling loudly on a stove.

"Girl, Lavonda blind and deaf. Frankie gon' take her to the cleaners."

"Hell, he take her to the *bank*," says another. "Fuckin' *Accounts Closed*."

In a corner, a quiet woman snaps the shrimp shells at the sharp hook in their tails and hums off-key. Her big, dark eyes are half-closed. Her fingers are raw. Angry red. A Lysol-and-pepper smell swarms the room.

I order some Kung Pao Chicken.

On the way home I stop at the Kroger's on Montrose for a six-pack of beer. At the pharmacy, in the rear of the store, next to the frozen fish, two pale, thin men wait in line. One thumbs through *This Week in Texas*. "William tells me AZT is cheaper now over at Walgreen's," his friend says.

"Sweet William. How are his platelets?"

"Pathetic."

* * *

For Sale.
Apartment for Rent.
Must Liquidate.

While I've walked in the fog of my grief a whole community has dwindled around me.

As I park my car by the curb, a young man pulls down a yellowed shade in a cracked apartment window across the street. Somewhere down the block a radio plays "Hang On, Sloopy."

Sno King clatters like a riot. I take a beer and my chicken to the far end of my garage, where sometimes it's quieter than it is in the house. I discovered this once coming home late from a blues club. I didn't want to wake Jean or risk pissing her off. I spent the night curled like a puppy in a nest of garden hoses. Afterward, anticipating other late nights and the need to bunk out here, I bought a sleeping bag and a pillow for just such occasions. I hung a mirror on a nail and filled a large tin tub with water so I could shave. Sometimes a cricket, flaccid as a penis, wound up trapped in the tub, floating on an island of Gillette Foamy. Spiders rappelled up rolls of insulation next to a dirty workbench. Roaches skittered over wrenches, screwdrivers, drills. But I always slept well. Somehow—an acoustical quirk—Sno King's noise was muffled by the thin, splintery walls.

I raise my bottle in the dark. "Sleep well, my love." I can't see her but I feel her. "I won't disturb you anymore. Promise."

12.

For Ray's driving lesson I've chosen Freedmen's Town, a mostly Black neighborhood northeast of Montrose, not far from the Magnolia Blossom Cemetery. The streets are narrow but largely straight, and the traffic is light.

Driving through here, I've sometimes drawn fierce stares from daytime porch-sitters but I've never worried. So many cheerful mothers live in the area. I've seen them watching their kids in the yards.

The Town—a few blocks long—was founded by ex-slaves shortly after the Civil War. It used to have filling stations, dry-goods stores, and nightclubs, but now it's a cluster of dilapidated rent houses threatened by bulldozers and high-flying redevelopment. Here and there, its old brick streets bleed through the asphalt. It's possible to feel connected to the past here more thoroughly than anywhere else in the city.

"Take a left here," I tell Ray. "Watch this corner. It's a sharp one. Okay, when you hit the brake, don't stomp. Pump it a little. Gently. That's it."

We pass a dusty brick building in a field of weeds, the old city-county hospital named for Jefferson Davis. It's been closed for years. Jagged glass teeth are all that remain of its windows.

I take us past an Asian grocery and a row of wooden houses. A hand-lettered sign droops on a dead yellow lawn: "Big Bad Dog."

Hip-hop shouts from open windows. Glass breaks somewhere—a porch light shattered with a rock? Laughter cartwheels down the block.

In the near distance, downtown Houston glimmers, peach and amber. A sumpy sulfur smell rises from tall, moist grass and froggy mudholes, seeping, exposed to the sky.

"Stay off the shoulder. There's broken glass up there. That's it. You're doing fine."

"It turns real smooth," Ray says. "Unc's Bookmobile is a little hard to handle. No power steering."

"You're going to have to get a Maserati or something if you're going to impress the girls."

He grins.

"You want to try parking?"

"Sure."

"Pull in over there where it says Mount Carmel Baptist Church."

I catch a whiff of pork chops in the air. They're overdone. Fried okra. Ray whips the car into a wide slot between two faint yellow lines. He jerks us to a stop.

"Sorry," he says.

"Remember. Pump the brakes."

We sit with the windows down. In vacant lots all around us crickets creak like heavy old doors.

"Where are we?" Ray asks.

"The Fourth Ward. Freedmen's Town."

"It's seen its better days, huh?"

"Yeah. It used to be the heart and soul of Black Houston. Then the city ran a freeway through here and chopped it all up."

Ray wipes his eyes.

"Hey. What is it, Ray?"

"I'm sorry, Mr. Palmer."

"You did great. Really. You'll get the hang of the brakes."

"No. I mean, it's not the brakes."

"Your dad?"

He nods. He sits still for a minute. Then he says, "For months, my mom and me, we've been so anxious about him, you know? It's the first time someone close to me has been real sick. The first time I've had to think about him . . . maybe dying. Scares hell out of me."

"I know."

"And of course it makes me think about my *own* death . . . I mean, I've always known I'd kick off someday, but . . . "

"It's *real* for you now?"

"Yeah." He's quiet for a moment. He looks around the neighborhood. "Hell. Cities die, too, I guess, don't they? *Nothing's* going to last."

Someone pounds a horn down the street. Tires squeal.

"You've got to cruise with the changes, Ray. That's all you can do."

"Yeah." He smiles at me, poised, handsome—too young to feel this bad. What would a wise father tell him?

"All right then. What do you say? Another spin around the block?"

"No thanks, Mr. Palmer." He rubs his cheeks. "I think that's enough for today."

"Okay. You're going to be a fine driver, Ray."

We change places. With the car still in park I pump the brakes. Once. Twice. Testing myself.

13.

I still meet the Thuots once a week. Their oldest son, Kim—sixteen, and with a good command of English—submitted one of the job applications I'd brought the family and got a cashiering spot at a Circle K convenience store. Last Wednesday, the Thuots spent his first check on roast duck and rice and invited me to dinner.

I toasted them with a bottle of cheap Italian wine I'd bought. In Tuscan folklore, I told them, water's linked to filth (pissing) while alcohol, *fa buon sange*, makes for good blood.

I brought them some shrimp from Water Under the Bridge. "And," I said, "you won the raffle at Cal's Bookstore."

"The what?" asked Mr. Thuot.

"Free gifts."

"My goodness. How did this happen?"

"I entered your name. Here." Cal had been furious. He'd hoped a regular customer would be hooked into spending hundreds of dollars in the store. Worried about his competition—the encroaching chain stores—he wasn't in the mood to let the Thuots come in and choose their own prizes. "What do they care? Do they even read? Just give them these."

Now Mr. Thuot stared, confused, at the stack I'd handed him: a deck-repair manual, a shipbuilder's guide, *The Bra Book*, and Mamie Eisenhower.

The family unpacked its gongs. We rang the gongs several times to celebrate Kim's good fortune. I gave him six free passes to the Shamrock.

"The children," said Mr. Thuot. "May their skies be high!"

We filled our fragile cups to the brim.

* * *

Tonight birthday candles in paper lantern shells float down the bayou at dusk: a festival of lights—"The Bayou Beckons," the city calls it, a celebration of Fiestas Patrias, Mexico's Independence Day, as well as a remembrance of families who died in Hiroshima (each flickering flame in the mist a token of loss).

Flowers and wooden crosses mark Chatitio's drowning, Roberto's disappearance.

Mariachi music echoes in the trees. Fireworks break like eggs against the sky. *Gritos*—shouts of independence—carry on hot breezes. Beneath an old bridge, Asian priests ask children to send their thoughts to Heaven, to those who once wore cloaks of fire.

A young Japanese couple cuddles in the grass. The woman is pregnant. I remember an old Ashanti folktale. *In the beginning women bore no children. One day a python asked a man and woman who came to bathe in his river if they had any offspring. "No," they replied unhappily. "Bring your friends to my woods," the python instructed them. "I'll make the women conceive." The couple did as they were told. When the people had gathered, the snake said, "Each couple must stand toe to toe." He slithered into the river and drew a mouthful of water. Then he sprayed the water on the bellies of all the men and women and told them to lie together that night in warm leaf-beds on the ground. Nine months later the world knew birth and desire.*

I scramble down a steep, dusty bank. Coors cans rust in the mud. Condoms. Cigarette butts. The lapping and sucking of water meeting land. Separate worlds. I toss a stone into the river. It makes a sound like a voice, a voice almost decipherable to me from a realm beyond my own.

Another stone. Another voice. I've started a conversation. A boisterous family.

"Where are you?" I whisper to the water. Reeds rattle like maracas.

"I don't believe in ghosts," Julio told me last year in one of our earliest interviews. "But I pray to God each night they'll leave us the hell alone."

A lump of moss, dark green and blue, as long as a woman's gown, wraps a broken limb in the stream. Every American city claims some version of the "disappearing woman." It's a common folktale.

A beautiful hitchhiker in a satin dress, pacing the shore of a lake, hails a passing driver. A disheveled young girl, seeking a ride.

Wet dreams.

Pick her up and she'll give you her address. But on the way there she shimmers and fades, leaving just a trace of moisture in your car. When you reach her street you find the ruins of a stately mansion where people died long ago. Or you find nothing at all.

* * *

South Ruthven Street is deserted this late at night. Quiet. Pretty, lined with elms. I used to come here every evening. Then I joined Little Vegas after work, dealing cards, hoping to starve my grief. I avoided the graveyard altogether.

"One of my families is in trouble," I tell my father's chiseled name. His headstone is chilly. Gray. The cemetery smells of mint and wild onion. Frogs chirp in the bayou by the road. "I don't know what to do about it. I just . . . thought I needed to tell you."

Some flying creature—a misguided bird, a bat—flitters in the trees.

Paper plates have blown against the stones. Napkins, cups. The Day of the Dead. I've missed it. Families must have been here, sharing meals with their lost ones. A candle in a cracked glass container (with the Virgin of Guadalupe painted on the glass) tilts on a mound of fresh dirt next to three or four paper-wrapped roses and a handful of yellow marigolds.

I say hello to my mother, stored neatly here like a small, brittle ornament.

Faint light in the east. The moon. In just a few hours, the sun will rise there, illuminating this wild little garden.

Twigs litter Jean's plot. I kneel. Given the chance, later, the day of the wreck, we would have kissed and made up. I know it. "We always did, didn't we?" I say.

Dried apple leaves crackle in the grass. I left them for Jean on my last visit here, months ago. "Always," I say, and for the first time since the funerals I weep.

14.

"Draw. Nothing wild." I'm dealing a fresh pack.

"See you, raise a dollar."

"I'll take three."

"Dealer needs two."

Ray circles Loop 610. We're all sitting in Cal's Bookmobile, gliding on the freeway in a glass-bottomed boat.

"Cal, man, I'm so glad we invited you," Tony says. "Now, *this* is the way to play!"

Cal grins. He'd suggested the Bookmobile and take-out pizza, a moveable feast, as a way of adding zest to the game. "Keep moving, Ray," he calls up front. "You're doing just fine."

Ray squirms a little behind the wheel. "Which way, Unc?"

"*Any* way. Just drive."

Houston, perched precariously on a gumbo of cracked soil and dry red clay, erupts in blue and green, tan and white. L-shapes, quarried stone (granite, marble, basalt), recessed windows, enclosed sidewalks, circles, triangles, squares—fissures into which people wedge their sighing bodies, moving up and down or deep underground, whispering, laughing, lying.

"Low spade splits the pot."

"Six and ten, no help . . . "

Eighty bucks in the hole, I fold early and slide up front next to Ray. "Cal paying you for this gig?"

"Naw. I need the practice."

He's a pretty good driver though he still takes his curves too fast. "How's your dad?" I ask.

"Home now. Mom's looking after him. That makes them both happy but he's still really sick."

One thing about families: beyond a certain point, I've learned, there's nothing much you can do for them.

Kim Thuot counting nickels in his store.

Julio Zamora waiting to be deported. Scott heard he was apprehended yesterday along with a family named Muñoz, with whom he'd been hiding in a house in the Fifth Ward. The cops caught him trying to break into his old place and cart off the washer and dryer.

I haven't been able to speak to him or the kids. My little web-slinger. Scott says there won't be a chance to see them before they leave.

Lira has been transferred to solitary confinement in a women's unit up near Huntsville.

I've read that divers have discovered a female manatee in the bayou, a dolphin, a red-bellied pacu—a native of South America, related to piranhas—an octopus, an armored catfish, a school of mullet, a Rio Grande perch . . .

No Roberto.

Take me home. Please. I need to go home. But I fear I'll disappear—a shower of water—before we get there.

"Full house!" Tony waves his cards.

Ray turns to see. He nearly swerves off the road. "Whoa there," I say. I reach over and steady the wheel for him.

The men razz him and he laughs. He's blushing. "Where should I go?" he asks me. "I'm running out of ideas."

"Try a left at the off-ramp," I say.

Tony's still crowing.

"Here?"

"Sure. You're doing fine." The city looks splendid. We're heading east now. With any luck we'll see the sun rise.

PART THREE

TOMBSTONE TELEVISION
1995

1.

Pedro Alcala died of influenza in November 1922 at the age of three-and-a half—so said an overworked general practitioner in the Houston barrio where Pedro's mother had given birth to him. Two hours after the informal funeral service Pedro awoke in his coffin. The gravedigger heard him crying.

He dropped out of school in the eighth grade. He told me this a few years ago, when I first listened to his story. "Cain't teach nothing to a dead man," he said. As a dropout he spent his days hanging around movie houses. "The movies was still pretty new back then. Flashy lights, sexy ladies. I figgered, whatever problems in the world, the movies can fix 'em."

After a tour of duty in Belgium during the Second World War he returned to Houston and devoted his life to erecting a monument in the boneyard where he'd nearly been buried.

Kewpie dolls, deer figurines, tapestries adorn his dusty grave, an old, abandoned stone with the lettering worn away. He'd found it in the cemetery's back lot and moved it to this spot. He's even hooked up a portable television set in a *gruta* in the middle of the stone, running a triple-ply cord to an outlet box behind a nearby mausoleum. The box was supposed to have been part of an outdoor lighting system never completed. Pedro discovered it still had juice.

91

I met him shortly after interring my family here in the Magnolia Blossom Cemetery. The groundskeeper warned me about Pedro: "He's a little spooky. Unnerves a few of our older visitors but you'll get used to him."

After we'd introduced ourselves and I'd told Pedro why I was there (I was standing in the rain that day clutching a dozen roses) he asked about my "people." "Was it their time to go?"

"Is it *ever* time to go?" And that's the last we've spoken about my family.

"So you live here?" I asked him incredulously.

"Where you think *you're* going to end up, man? I'm just saving a little time."

I dropped by to see him much more often once the Thuots moved away. They went to Dallas when Kim got a job with the Southland Corporation, overseeing a dozen 7-Eleven stores in north Texas. I was pleased they'd become the beneficiaries of American mobility but I missed them. The gaps in my days grew longer. So I made regular stops to check on Pedro.

This afternoon he's sitting on his mound watching *Wheel of Fortune*.

"Hey," I say.

"Hey. You look beat, bud." He's wearing thin black jeans, an old pair of sneakers and a white cotton shirt, sparsely buttoned.

"Fending off creditors," I admit. "How 'bout you? What's up?"

"Got me some angel hair and some Christmas lights." He shows me a box. "Old lady over in River Oaks tossed 'em in the trash. Don't know if the lights'll work. Thought I'd string 'em up around the TV."

A Styrofoam to-go container, stained with soy sauce, lies crumpled at his feet. "You getting enough to eat?" I ask.

"Tell you what I need, man's, a can opener." He lifts a can of pork and beans out of a soft paper sack. "Shit don't do me no good like this. Snapped my pocketknife on one the other day."

"All right. I'll fix you up next time. You have enough blankets?"

"Yeah." He points to the screen. "This chick kills me."

"Pretty," I say.

He grins slyly. "No doubt. You gettin' any, George? You lookin' mighty antsy these days."

He thinks women are the only worries a "youngster" like me could possibly grapple with in this crazy bayou city. I asked him once if he had family of his own. He scratched his ear and didn't say anything for a minute. Then: "Well. Yeah. Guess I did. Couple of kids."

"Where are they?"

Another silence. "All I know is they ain't here no more. Neither is their mother."

Now he coughs into his hands. "Refinery smoke," he wheezes, watching me watch him. "Blowin' in from the Gulf. Pisser today. It'll pass."

"All right, man." I slap his knee. "I'll bring you a can opener soon."

On the television a housewife from Gainesville, Florida wins ten thousand dollars and a car.

"Watch yourself," I say.

"Shit. Ain't no harm come to a man what's already dead."

2.

Rooting around in my desk drawer at work, looking for a stapler, I run across an ace of spades with the corner bent, a remnant of our now-defunct poker games. Scott's retired. Tony took a job managing an alternative weekly. Ed has remarried and is now a devoted homebody.

Cal left the bookstore to Ray and moved to Tucson where he said the high, dry air was good for his health. Ray sold the stock and turned the store into a shop specializing in engineering and automotive publications. Unlike his uncle, he's a workaholic and I don't see him much anymore, not since I helped him arrange his dad's burial in the Magnolia Blossom. (I'm convinced Cal retired early prompted by his brother's ordeal. In his last year at the store all he talked about was easing his stress.) I *do* occasionally see the Bookmobile on the road. Ray's using it as his personal vehicle. It's a wonder the thing still works—like my old Beast (I still think of my beater as "the Beast").

A year ago, Penrose relented and moved me from obits to small features. Someone had told him about O. Henry's column in early Houston newspapers, colorful sketches of city life. He decided we could use something like that—"as long as you keep it *positive*, hear me?"

It was a challenge. I started a bi-monthly column, "Tales from the Bayou City." I did fluff pieces on *Quinceaneras*, Hanukkah celebrations, mixed-race weddings (*that* one was "probably going to get us killed," Penrose said).

It turns out, the day I went to buy Pedro a can opener a small fire broke out in a shirt factory behind the supermarket. I stood in the parking lot with the other happy shoppers watching firemen scurry up ladders. (Disaster makes people pretty happy if they're not directly involved in it.) I hadn't known a shirt factory existed at that spot. I asked around. Were other sweatshops tucked away nearby? It might make a column though I doubted I could find something good to say.

The manager of a nearby noodle factory, a middle-aged Chinese man who'd once worked at a button plant on a side street just off West Gray, said, "Sure. All around us. What you look for, you look for steamed-up windows, especially on hot days when the windows should be open. Boarded-up buildings with a little steam spitting through cracks in their walls—yessiree. Dead give-away."

Once I started looking, I saw the nailed boards and the tell-tale plumes everywhere: above icehouses, shoe stores, auto parts suppliers. Next to the Bluebird Circle Shop and St. Vincent de Paul. I made notes and developed contacts on the streets, like a real investigative reporter. I dreamed of slipping like a spy inside a crime scene, winning a Pulitzer, the love of a good woman, and pulling a whole new family around me.

***

"Pedro, you ever work in a sweatshop?"

On his television a jumpy young weatherman says, "Cooler tomorrow."

"Sure. Me and all my friends did. Back in the thirties—"

"You were a *kid* in the thirties."

"A *workin'* kid, jack. Folks'd kill you for a dime, those days. I 'member these cardboard signs in the shop, all over the walls: 'No Home Work.' We couldn't take the cloth home and sew on it there. Ever'thing had to be done in the shop. It's a big joke, anyways, 'cause none of us, not even the adults, could afford a sewin' machine at home."

"And here we are near the end of the twentieth century. Nothing's changed."

From where we're sitting, in the northeast corner of the graveyard, we can see the Texas Commerce Bank building downtown, seventy-five stories, a correlated diamond pattern of rose and Barre granite. Its streaky windows blaze like tungsten bulbs.

"Poor folks still gotta work they asses off. *That* much hasn't changed," Pedro agrees. "But a whole lot else is differ'nt. Don't kid yourself."

"Like what?"

"I 'member 'Whites Only' signs in the Weingarten's store over on Almeda Street. Dig? I 'member Black folks comin' to the Messkins in the shops, real polite-like, askin' us to join 'em in the sit-ins at the lunch counters. 'You ain't white, neither,' they'd tell us. And they was right."

"Did you do a lunch counter?"

"Couple. The Texas Southern students, smart little whips from the law school over there, they led the charge. Brave fellas. But really, it was baseball finally broke the color line in Houston."

I hadn't heard this before. "How?"

"They wasn't any Major League teams in the South, see, till long about 1960 or so," Pedro says. "When the Buffs started here—later they's the Colt 45s and finally the Astros, that's when they'd forgot how to hit the damn ball—anyways, when other teams come down to play 'em, what was the city gonna do? You couldn't put a made guy like Willie Mays up in a segregated hotel. Make Houston look bad to all them fancy-pantsed Northerners."

Busted shoes, cigarette lighters, condoms and pantyhose float down the bayou, past Pedro's grave.

"I'll tell you another way the city's changed."

"Tell me."

"It's going to hell."

"How?"

"I know it watchin' the funerals here. Gettin' cheaper. Shabby damn boxes. No handles for the whatcha-call-'em, the pallbearers to carry 'em with. Might as well be wrappin' these poor motherfuckers in tinfoil."

He doubles over, coughing.

"Man, I don't like the sound of that," I say.

"It'll pass."

"You got to keep breathing for me, Pedro. Who else is going to tell me these stories?"

"That's right," he says. "*I'm* gone, the history of this sorry-ass neighborhood's gone."

3.

One of my street contacts pointed out to me a Mr. Ho, a pudgy man with glazed-looking skin, the manager of the shirt factory where the fire had been. I caught him one morning on the wooden steps leading to the only entrance I could see into the building, a door covered with steel sheeting. It was as wide as an NFL linebacker. Mr. Ho wouldn't speak to me at first. But finally I wore him down with my repeated use of the word "sweatshop."

"Is not sweatshop," he insisted.

"What do you call it then?"

"Garment factory. Is garment factory." He scratched his shiny nose. His eyes flicked back and forth, swift as two hummingbirds.

"On the street I've heard rumors that half your employees are underage," I said. "Is that true?"

"Is not true."

"Can you prove that? Will you give me a tour?"

"No tour."

"What's your pay scale?"

"Very good. Very competitive."

"Not what I heard."

"What you heard?"

"You pay much less than minimum wage."

"Hear that where?"

"On the street."

He leaned over the wooden railing and dropped a gob of spit on the parking lot below us. "Street is filthy. Filthy dirty words on the street."

"If you have nothing to hide, sir, I don't see why I can't—"

"Work to do. Excuse me." He tapped seven times on the door. Three big men let him in. They barred my way. A blast of hot air. Scalding steam.

An hour later I came back. I tapped seven times on the door. The big men nearly threw me off the stairs. Mr. Ho stood over me as I collected myself in the parking lot. "Whatsa matter, you? Go Home. Take care your family. Let me do my work so you have nice clean shirt to wear, okay?"

**

I don't even know if Penrose would've taken the story. All he said was, "Be careful."

And one night: "Why are you always working so late, George? Our circulation isn't wide enough to justify your efforts. Go home. Take care of your family."

4.

Pedro's hunched above his grave coughing so hard he can barely breathe. I drop the blanket I've brought him and walk him to my car. "No, George, I cain't leave my TV settin' here!" he wheezes. "I've never left my TV!"

"I'll unplug it for you and store it in my trunk. It'll be okay."

"Dopeheads'll swipe it. They sneak in here at night to do they deals, you know. Fuck they johns. Pass out. I'm tellin' you, city's going to hell."

"Easy, now." I help him into the car.

The neighborhood clinic, on Dallas Street, sits across an alley from a chipped brick building with a hand-lettered sign in an upper window: "Bombay Films."

Teenagers fill the clinic's waiting room. Tattooed and pierced. One's eating Fritos. He keeps dropping the bag. He looks like he's asleep except every now and then when he nibbles a chip.

An orange-haired boy is sharing a can of RC Cola with a girl whose lips are purple. "It was the real deal, man," he tells her. "We could actually *taste* the meth on each other's *tongues*." At his feet sits a duffel bag bearing a chewed-on pipe and several bags of Ramen.

I flash my Blue Cross card. The receptionist hands me some forms to fill out for Pedro. The papers feel damp in the small, humid room.

Pedro's huffing beside me. "Is gone," he says. "Poof!"

"What are you talking about?"

"The neighborhood. *Look* at this shit."

Across the room, a boy says to a nervous friend of his (leg like a jackhammer bouncing up and down), "No bullshit. He'll help me off the streets."

"He's a dealer, man. How's he gonna help you off the streets?"

"Brother *connected*. He ain't like them preachers at the soup kitchens. Those ass-wipes just like us, man."

"How you mean?"

"They got nowhere to go, *either*."

Forty-five minutes later a young doctor helps me guide Pedro to a leather table in a little room. On the wall is a poster: a cut-away drawing of a woman's uterus, the fallopian tubes branching like wings on either side of it. It looks like a B-47 bomber.

"Undo your shirt, please," the doctor says to Pedro. He's blond and horsey-looking. Pedro's stopped coughing. When he touches his buttons, puffs of dust rise from his fingers.

After a brief examination the doctor motions me into the hall. The place smells of Mercurochrome, wet tennis shoes. "You're this fellow's guardian?"

"Not legally. I look after him some."

"Where's he live?"

"In a graveyard."

"Homeless, then?"

"I guess . . . yes, you could say that." Though it seems to me Pedro knows exactly where he belongs.

"He's not getting enough liquids. The dry throat, the coughing, and so on. Is there some way you can make sure he gets several glasses of fresh water daily?"

"Sure."

"There's a bigger problem."

"What's that?"

"Asthma. Pretty severe, I'm afraid. God knows what he's exposed to, living outdoors all the time. Probably has several allergies. I'd like to put him on a breather for half an hour, open up his lungs. Can you wait?"

"I'll wait."

"I'll set it up then."

The light's too bright in Pedro's room. He's blinking like a stuck traffic signal. "I'm missing *Jeopardy*," he says.

"I'll get you back soon."

"It's half over! George?"

"Yes?"

"What if someone steals my Christmas bulbs?"

"We've got to get you well, man."

The kids' talk in the waiting room depresses me so I wait outside in the alley behind the clinic. It smells of urine. The door to the building abutting the clinic is open, revealing a steep wooden stairway, crooked, cracked, water-damaged. I look for steam but don't see any.

At the top of the stairs there's another sign for "Bombay Films" by a frosted-glass door. Next to it, a torn black-and-white poster: Marlon Brando kissing Maria Schneider.

The economic life of the city, pumping away.

I return to the clinic to check on Pedro. He's huffing into a cardboard tube on a machine bearing an uncanny resemblance to a carpet cleaner. I give him a thumbs-up and he scowls. In the waiting room, the girl with purple lips slowly licks Madonna's face on the cover of *Vogue*.

Back in the alley, a woman approaches "Bombay Films" wearing a yellow mini-skirt and spiked black heels. A Walkman rides her waist. She flicks a cigarette into an open trash bin and starts up the stairs. Halfway up, her left heel catches an exposed nail and she stumbles. "Goddammit!" she shouts, spotting me. She grabs her ankle. "These your stairs? I'll sue you bastards!" She whips off her shoe.

The door at the top of the landing groans open. A paunchy, bald man wearing cowboy boots. Thick glasses. "Are you the dancer from Haughty Bitch Showgirls?" he calls down the stairs. "April?"

She pulls a pack of Marlboro Lights from her right skirt pocket. "Guzman?"

"Yeah. Call me Goose." He appraises her frankly. "They told me you had *tits*, April."

"Fuck you." She climbs the stairs and shoves past him into his office.

He adjusts his glasses and studies me. "You the new guy? From the distributors downtown? Barney? Beatty?"

"Not me."

"Come on up. *Cup of Flesh* is ready to go."

"I'm not the guy."

He fiddles again with his glasses.

"I'm waiting for a friend at the clinic."

"Oh? Blood test? Your buddy getting married? Need some stag films?"

"No thanks."

"All right then." He wags his head. "Change your mind, I got some stills here that'll dilate your fuckin' pupils."

***

I reconnect Pedro's television to the outlet behind the mausoleum. He settles down for *The Price is Right*. "I *tol'* you I was gonna miss *Jeopardy*. Mr. Ace Reporter." His voice is thin. Scared, I think. "You'd expeck he'da figgered that out." The doctor gave me an inhaler for him and I plug it into his mouth.

The doc also slipped me a packet of Accolate tablets. "Twice a day with lots of liquids. Can you bring him back here, end of the week? I'd like to check him."

"Sure."

"You can keep an eye on him, right? In case something goes wrong with the medications?"

"Absolutely," I say, never more aware of the truth. "He's pretty much family now."

5.

On Friday I'm waiting in the alley while Pedro huffs for Doctor Horsey. April appears in Guzman's stairwell wearing only a bra and panties. Grape lipstick. Small, powdered breasts. "I'm auditioning for Goose's latest Western epic," she says. "*Saloon Sluts*. He's up there in the studio arranging the cactus."

I smile at her.

"If I get the part I get to die. Got a light?"

"Sorry, no."

"You work at the clinic or what?"

"Newspaperman."

"True crime? Scandal and divorce? I love that stuff."

"More like community service. Local history."

"I got some history for you."

"Oh?"

"Pancho Villa raped my grandmother."

I don't know what to say.

"When he crossed the border, you know?"

"That right?"

"Granny cut his pecker off with a Bowie knife."

"Really? You're sure about that?"

"Sure I'm sure. She used to let me play with it. She kept the little feller in a pickle jar down in Harlingen."

***

Horsey hands me some Flonase and Albuterol. "These are samples. They should last him a month or so. If his breathing's still labored then, I'll write you a prescription for more."

Pedro's sucking on a tube—like he's gasping for the city's last sweet breath.

"He'll never get better," the doctor advises me softly. "But maybe we can keep him from getting worse for a while."

6.

About a month after my last encounter with Mr. Ho another fire broke out in the shirt factory. I got the news on the street. Three women, all in their teens, collapsed of smoke inhalation on the floor because the door was locked and they couldn't get out.

One morning, from the supermarket parking lot, I called to Mr. Ho. He was standing at the top of his stairs. "You!" he said, jabbing a finger at me. "Interloper! *Bad* man!"

"You have a statement, Mr. Ho?"

"Door never *had* a lock on it till you come snooping around asking nosy question! Now city shut us down. *Your* fault!"

I felt only relief that the women hadn't died. "I'm sorry for your troubles," I said.

"Whatsa matter, you? You don't like nice clean shirt? What the world be without nice clean shirt?"

***

Penrose insisted I stop working late, stop chasing so hard after stories. "No one reads anything these days but the damn headlines. And *those* they don't understand," he grumbled.

I settled into a dull routine.

At home, in the wee hours of the morning when I couldn't sleep, when I'd tired of flipping through family photos, when Sno King was *thwacking* away, I'd watch the local cable access channel.

Guzman produced its highest-rated show, "Naked Sports with April Blow." April sat topless behind a flimsy desk talking baseball, hockey, squash. I loved to hear her say "squash." Mornings after, I could never remember last night's scores. All I saw was 0-0.

7.

Once a week now I bring Pedro some fresh Ozarka water. I've made him a chart so he'll know when he's taken his pills. He marks it with a pencil.

This evening I bring him some beer to go with his supper: a stick of jerky, lightly salted, two lemons and an orange. I sit and drink with him.

"They just closed a bunch of refineries east of town," he says. "City goin' through some panty-twistin' money shit. But it makes the air cleaner. Ain't used my inhaler all week."

"Good," I say. I gaze across the graveyard, past Ray's dad to my family's stones. It's the sixth anniversary of the accident and I'm blue.

A Mickey Mouse mask, a gold ceramic owl and a laminated poster of a unicorn line Pedro's dusty *gruta*. He points to a muddy pool choked with garbage over by the war veterans' plots. Plastic US flags rain-beaten to the ground. "Lots of new stuff floatin' down the bayou this week. Socks. Broken toys."

Still no Roberto. After all these years. He belongs to the stream now.

"Gonna do me some rearrangin'," Pedro says. With his left foot he shoves the owl closer to the mask. "Fella cain't let hisself get bored."

We decide to watch a movie on his tombstone television: *Dancing in the Dark*, about a down-and-out actor, starring William Powell. Every so often Pedro wipes dust from the screen.

After a while my attention drifts to the trees, the mint smell, the cooing of night-birds. "I think you've got the right idea, Pedro."

"How's that?"

I grab another beer. "Tending your own grave."

"Ah hell."

"One way or the other it's what we *all* do, right?"

"What the fuck you talkin' 'bout, George?"

"Working useless jobs. Losing our families."

"Aw man. You're a sad drunk." He watches me. "You need to get laid."

"No. Well, yes. But that's not what's creeping me out."

"What's creepin' you out is you own mopey self! You probably *stay* mopey even after you *been* laid."

"Sometimes."

"Mr. Ace Reporter. Sees Evil ever'where he turns. Wants to right the world's wrongs. That it?"

"You said it yourself. The neighborhood's gone."

"Shit. If it's anything I cain't stand, it's a sad drunk."

I shrug.

He cracks another beer. Downtown Houston twinkles in the distance. "Watch the damn movie," he says.

PART FOUR

BURYING THE BLUES
2000

1.

At two o'clock I found Spider Lammamoor on the porch of his house in the projects over on Dowling Street. Spider wore a green cotton shirt, unbuttoned to the waist, jeans with no belt, and no shoes. His skin, scarred, etched with wrinkles, was the deep dark color of balsam.

In his slender fingers he gripped a malt liquor can. Now and then he brought it to his lips. "Been doin' me some thinkin'," he said. I locked my Chrysler by the curb and joined him on the jagged porch. "Takes a long sit." He lifted the can. "And half-a-dozen quarts of this-here oil."

His voice always had a silty quality, hard for me to describe. Whenever I recorded Spider talking and tried to transcribe what he said, I faced the problem of rendering his dialect accurately without making it look, on the page, like some version of the old Amos and Andy patter, an offensive and condescending exercise in patronizing the man. After all, I was a privileged, educated white man, trained in formal English, trying to represent the speech patterns of a member of another social class and ethnic background. And, of course, as the young academics I knew warned me more and more, I was open to the charge of appropriating my subjects' voices for my own purposes.

It was tricky business—no business of mine at all, insisted the militant young scholars. The folklorist's/historian's dilemma.

"You're way ahead of me," I told Spider now. I handed him a six-pack of Colt 45s. "I brought these for you but—"

"Set 'em down. We'll put 'em to use." He reached inside his shirt and scratched his belly just below the stark outline of his ribs. Cicadas made a crazy racket in the trees.

"So what is it you been thinking about?" I said.

"This weekend."

"Good. You ready?"

Spider had been Houston's finest blues drummer but two years ago he'd simply quit. Recently, I'd talked him into performing again with a group of young musicians at the city's annual Juneteenth Celebration.

"I'm ready. But the world's changed, man."

"How do you mean?"

"Listen. Listen." Still clutching his can, Spider pointed past the trees. Fingered leaves curled in the heat. He indicated a long series of row houses behind the swaying limbs. Oak shadows waved across the house's dark bricks, a jigsaw of rich and shifting light. On one of the walls someone had painted muscular Black arms chained at the wrists.

I heard children laughing, cars backfiring and chugging on the Loop, north of Dowling Street. I wondered how many malt liquors Spider had consumed already.

Then he nudged my shoulder. "There it is," he said. "Hear it?"

A muffled throb from somewhere in the houses. An angry, rhythmic voice. "You mean the boom box?"

"Yeah! Rappin' shit. Kids today, man, they pissed off and mean. Listen to that *wham wham wham* all the time. None of the old tunes. Ain't no place for me here. Not no more."

"That isn't true," I said.

"My day come and gone."

"You wait and see this weekend. More people than ever love the blues." I offered him a cigarette. I didn't smoke but I always

114

carted a carton of Camels over here. He tended to relax after a few drags.

"*White* folks, you mean. Tourists."

"No. Not just."

"That's why *you* here, right? Blues be history now, ready for the museum. This weekend, people just stare at us: 'These motherfuckers played the blues. Listen. This is what it sounded like.'"

I laughed and reached for a beer. I'd first heard Spider two years ago at the Crackerbarrel Lounge, a zydeco dance hall. That night, old Black men in straw cowboy hats whirled teenage girls around a raised wooden platform. Onstage, a man with an aluminum washboard strapped to his chest set the pace. Spider nailed down a "chanky-chank" beat. "Happy New Year!" the accordion player yelled, though it was the middle of July. Pedro had just died. He'd simply stopped breathing one night, slumped in front of his grave. He didn't have far to go to embrace his final rest. I was grieving that night at the Crackerbarrel but the music was so lively it overwhelmed me. It made me feel I could start over—a new beginning *each minute*, with a fresh crack at romance and fortune. I hadn't felt that way in years. Hadn't *let* myself feel it.

And truth to tell, I was eager to start over after a rough series of movements left me more stranded than ever. The newspaper work had never helped me get ahead of my bills. In '96, I applied for an adjunct instructor position in the history department at Marion Junior College downtown. Right away, I learned that I *was* the history department. To say the school's humanities budget was small is to say Houston is a city of some proportion.

The last obit I wrote for the paper was for Penrose, dead of a coronary one Sunday morning on the eleventh green at Hermann Park golf course. I shed several grudging but genuine tears for the old dog.

Within a month of starting at the college I met a divorcee named Paula Barr. She was the office manager in the business school. Topping out at two dozen faculty members, the business school was healthy and robust.

Paula was clearly on the rebound from her ex, but lonely, horny, a little disoriented from the job change, I pointedly ignored all the signals (especially her constant, late-night phone calls to "her Jimmy," even after her Jimmy went to work for Aramco and moved to Saudi Arabia). Besides that, her two girls, Elissa and Jane, ten and nine, reminded me of Monica and Kate (teenagers by now!). It's possible I was still on the rebound from Monica and Kate, even after all these years. Paula and I moved in together. I gave up the house I'd shared with Jean. It should have been a sign to me that I was happier escaping Sno King than I was waking next to Paula in the mornings. Another sign: after Paula burst into my study one night, declared me a "stuffy old fart" and told me she was moving to New Orleans where her parents lived, I immediately missed Elissa and Jane more than their mother.

By then, though, I agreed with Paula: I was hopelessly dull. Bored. Already tired of teaching intro history and writing articles on land grants, treaties, ancient Texas wars, aiming to publish in an academic journal and get a raise.

One day, shortly after Paula left with the girls (man, I'd been *there* before!), I was listening to my car radio, trying not to think of anything. But Spider Lammamoor came into my head. *A history of the Houston blues.* What if I tried something along the lines of the great musicologist Alan Lomax? He'd gone to the Mississippi Delta in the early 1940s to record Muddy Waters on his farm. Something like *that*, I thought—*that* might invigorate me.

It was risky: a white man using the blues to enter Black culture. But hell, I was a native Houstonian, right, familiar with most of its neighborhoods, sensitive to cultural tensions. I'd done similar things in the past—with the Thuots, the Zamoras. With Kelly at the Casa. I figured I could avoid the pitfalls.

I went to the Crackerbarrel Lounge, asked around, but Spider had retired. For three consecutive nights I schmoozed with the club's owner. I swallowed half a dozen pitchers of pale foam masquerading as beer. Finally, the man gave me Spider's address.

I was lucky. Spider loved to talk. If I kept him pumped with smokes and juice the lanky old stickman would spin every tale he knew.

Already, since leaving the paper, I had produced two long articles on KCOH, Houston's only all-Black radio station, now defunct. In the forties and fifties, it broadcast live from Emancipation Park, Shady's Playhouse, Club Ebony, and the El Dorado. The DJs—King Bee, Daddy Deepthroat, Mister El Toro—played dangerous, hip-grinding tunes. The white folks called them "race records." The term "rhythm and blues" hadn't been coined yet.

In the past two years, I'd spent whole afternoons at the public library, flipping through photos of old neighborhoods. Black Houston—in crackling, sepia tones—hanging her head (in the shape of stooping brown magnolias), tapping her feet (in the *splat* of withered peaches pelting heat-blasted ground), dancing (in the swirl of a Cadillac fin in the sun).

This was "Mama Houston." Spider's name for her. Loud and sweaty, sexy as a stripper, breathing hot and fast so her kids would shuck their shirts. Mama Houston—drunk on dewberries, ripe green apples; dizzy on her own delicious poisons, car exhaust, shit and ash and rust. She doesn't always know what's best for her kids but she loves them all, smothers us all, in her large and steamy arms.

Eighteen months ago, in our first recorded session, Spider told me about the dark days in 1945 when J. C. Petrillo, president of the American Federation of Musicians, had banned recording on the grounds that jukeboxes would put his union out of business.

"Damn near killed the city blues, man," Spider said. "Didn't get shit, playin' live. *Needed* those contracts, eb'n though the record man cain't be trusted."

A few months ago, I asked him why he'd retired.

Spider scratched his belly. "We's playin' one night down on Scott Street, middle of the summer, real hot, you know. Fight busted out. Fellow shot me in the shoulder." He raised his right arm gingerly: a long, broken wing. "Kinda put a kink in my flamacue."

I pressed him. Was he unable to play now? No. He asked for a second cigarette, another sip of beer. The wound had healed all right. It was just a matter of confidence.

Night after night, then, I drove him to some of the fancy new clubs in the Heights where middle-class kids, both Black and white, tried to keep the old riffs alive. Once they recognized the old bluesman, they fawned over Spider, listened, rapt, to his stories of the past. Finally, I persuaded him to take the stage again with some of this fresh new blood.

He hand-picked four mates: piano, bass, lead and rhythm guitars. The band had been rehearsing in a warehouse maintained by the physical plant over at the college.

Now Spider seemed determined to mothball his cymbals again.

"You'll knock 'em dead. I promise," I said.

"They laughin' at me."

"Who?"

A white Ford Mustang—a '68 model, I guessed—sporting mag wheels and tinted gold windows cruised the street, bass and drums ratcheting out of its speakers. It paused by my Chrysler then lurched away down the block.

"These young punks with they high-topped sneakers and back-assward baseball caps, that's who. To them, I'm a old coot. What I *don't* want to be—" He opened another can. "—is a Tom."

"A Tom? What do you mean?"

"I mean—I'm astin' you now—is the blues the white man's *fashion*? College kids with they scholarships and Daddy's business cards—it's hip for them to go slummin' now in the blues joints? Watch Uncle Tom tappin' out a beat to please the new young masters?"

"Whoa. Spider. Spider, where are you getting this?" A siren moaned in the distance. "Who've you been talking to? I thought we were friends."

"Me too." He scratched the back of his ear with a pull tab.

"Well then, we *are*, right? Spider, I love what you do. Period. It has nothing to do with Black and white. I mean, the *music* does, its polyrhythms—" No: I was veering into "stuffy old fart" territory. "Okay, you know. I'll back off if you want me to. I'll—"

"No no no." Spider struck a match. He lit a Camel. "It's just that, some of the young guys in the band, they see more whites than brothers in the clubs and they wonder what's going on. And I look around *me*." A couple of boys across the street wearing baggy yellow shorts and Jordan shoes were laughing and slapping hands. Silver chains bounced around their necks. "These kids, to them the blues is Lawrence Fuckin' Welk. Ast 'em 'bout music, it's gangsta this, gangsta that. I'm just a no-account old fool."

"Well, that makes two of us," I said. I crumpled my empty can. "But the blues is going to be around, Spider, long after you and I and those kids are gone."

He grinned. "Yeah. Yeah, I hear *that*."

"All right, man. So. I'll stop by Friday?"

"Okey-doke. Bring me some smokes, awright?"

The Mustang circled the street again. A mighty orgasm shuddered in its speakers. I kept my eyes down, walking back to my car. The cruiser squealed away, swerving wildly past the projects and the shackled Black fists.

2.

On my way back to school I considered Spider's questions. Folklorists and historians—many of them white—*had* taken an urgent interest in the blues, following Alan Lomax's example. A lot of the leading blues players, nationwide, were dying or dead. It was true too that music was a fluid, culturally sensitive activity, changing with the times, and fewer kids nowadays seemed drawn to tradition.

But it was a long way from all this to "Uncle Tom."

I touched my radio button. "What's *wrong* with bigamy?" someone shouted: a call-in show. On another station, a young, grating DJ argued that Led Zeppelin was the greatest flowering of musical genius the Western world had ever witnessed.

Finally, I found Black Magic, an independent, unlicensed broadcast from somewhere in the city's Fifth Ward projects. Repeatedly, the police had tried to jam the broadcast or yank the show off the air but the operator—who identified himself only as "Black Magic What Comes in the Night"—eluded them. The story had been in all the papers. The people in the Fifth Ward—poor Blacks, mostly—hid and protected the man. At first he'd come on-air to read renter's complaints and to demand better city housing for the poor. Then he expanded his format, broadcasting police radio calls, accusing the cops of brutality and racism. Between editorial comments, he played local rappers.

The signal was weak: "You got the Black Magic here, Freedom Radio. We be checking in on the Pig-Line soon, see what Caveboy up to. The occupyin' army of the fat white race comin' to kidnap our fine young men, you dig? Oink. Oink oink. Any pigs out there? I know you be listenin', pigs."

The radio crackled. Another voice: "You better believe we're listening."

"Ah, we got us one! Got us a pig!" Black Magic shouted. "Say, Porky, tell me this: Why you occupyin' my neighborhood?"

"It's our job. Your listeners need to know that. We're here to serve and protect."

"Protect *who*, Caveboy?"

"The citizens of Houston."

"The *denizens* of Houston? Tell you what, pig, you crawl outta your cave, we might have us somethin' to talk about."

I would love to have found the man and brought him to my classroom. A quick lesson in contemporary American culture. One of my favorite exercises on the first day of each term was to ask my students, many of whom were internationals, to draw a world map. The students were always shocked to find they'd each placed their home—Venezuela, Italy, the Ivory Coast—in the maps' centers. None of their worlds looked alike, even remotely. Listening to Black Magic now, I figured few of Houston's *neighborhoods* looked alike anymore.

Black Magic played the Geto Boys: "I like bitches, all kinda bitches / to take off my shirt and pull down my britches."

You're going to be fine, I thought. Just be careful with Spider. Honest and respectful. You're *not* exploiting the man. It's important to trace the history of this music. If Lomax hadn't dragged his tape recorder under the willows, into the swamps, through hellish swarms of bugs, the world might never have heard "Dust My Broom" and that would be a tragedy for the world.

Just two summers ago I'd gone hunting Robert Johnson's famous crossroads in the Mississippi Delta. I was dismayed to find a Sonic Drive-In, a KFC, a Church's Chicken and a Fuel Mart blighting the mythic corner. No sign of Satan, just the devils of fast commerce.

Everything good gets lost if someone doesn't bother to save it.

On a dirt sidewalk, now, dozens of young Black men gathered in loose circles in front of a boxing gym. Idling at a stoplight I watched them feint and jab at the air. A boom box pulsed with a steady sexual rhythm, the same ebb and flow as birdsong and insect trills in the trees. Down the street, an old man tugged at the steel bars on a liquor store's bright purple windows. A scent of tar mixed with something else—a faint dead-animal smell, wafting up from Mama Houston's alleys. The light turned green. Somewhere, train cars clattered. I moved my foot off the brake. A thin boy, toothless, shirtless, slick with sweat, turned and gave me the finger.

***

I checked the "to-do" list in my office. Write a test for my freshman class, a stew of nationalities with basic reading and writing problems (the college budget didn't allow for separate English-as-a-second-language courses). And I had to call Paula. She'd lived in New Orleans for three years now and the girls' attachment to me had only grown stronger, as had my bond with them. With their dad overseas, out of reach, Elissa and Jane seem to have transferred their affection to the last man who'd stepped in as a father-figure for them. My tensions with Paula never weakened my ties to the girls. And I'd learned my lesson from the dance with Kelly, with Monica and Kate. Don't let go so easily. Paula didn't like it but the girls and I spoke regularly on the phone, and each summer they came to see me for a week.

I picked up the phone and punched Paula's number. From my tiny office window I saw Firebirds, Darts and Gremlins rush the freeway down the hill from the campus, past the main entrance and the faintly faded "Marion Junior College" sign. A few miles away, Life-Flite emergency helicopters circled the glass spires of the medical center.

Elissa answered on the fourth ring. Paula had taught her proper telephone etiquette. She was solemn and reserved until she recognized my voice. Then she shouted, "Jane has stinky underwear!" and I heard both girls laugh.

Mama was next door borrowing flour for dinner, Elissa said. I tried to pin her down about her summer schedule but she was manic with energy. I heard Jane running around the kitchen. Elissa giggled and bumped the receiver on the wall. I gave up. "Tell your mother I called, will you?"

"George, are we coming to see you?" she asked.

"Later this summer, sweetheart. Give your sister a kiss for me."

"*Ewww!*"

3.

After Paula left Houston, I'd moved into a small apartment on Jack Street, near the intersection of Richmond and Highway 59. It was in the Montrose neighborhood, just a few blocks from where I'd lived with Jean. That area of town always felt like home to me. The apartment manager, showing me around, assumed I was a newbie. He informed me that, before the AIDS epidemic, Montrose had been mostly gay, with an inflated reputation for debauchery. In fact, it was largely peaceful, tastefully landscaped and kept. Street people slept in alleys behind the 7-Elevens but that was true all over the city. On my block, the five or six people who stowed rags, blankets and bags in back of the dumpsters were friendly but withdrawn, embarrassed when asking for change.

On my way home from school, weaving through traffic, I half-listened to the radio news. Despite a strong showing last night against the Mets, the Astros had blown a double-header today. Damned Astros. Couldn't hit their way out of a paper bag.

At a stoplight on Westheimer a big, freckled fireman strolled into the intersection waving a black rubber boot. He was soliciting money for a city-fund-raiser. I lowered my window—a surge of hot air—and stuffed a dollar into the boot.

As I pulled my car onto Jack Street I noticed an old woman by the corner wearing a bulky tan sweater despite the heat. It had unraveled so much it looked like a tumbleweed. Her face was as dark as the fireman's boot. She shuffled around the block.

Maple leaves flapped like oily rags on branches stretched the width of the street. Cicadas whirred, loud rotary blades, in the tallest limbs.

My place was filled with K-Mart stuff. Paula had taken all her good furniture and I'd sold most of the items I'd had with Jean when Paula and I moved in together. I hadn't bothered to get any nice new things. Sometimes I thought about buying a five or ten gallon fish tank—angel fish and neon tetras maybe—an echo of my father's giant aquarium which I'd loved so much as a kid. But I figured its puny scale would just depress me. A major comedown from the past. An ineffective way to bury my blues.

I showered and shaved, worked on my freshman test for a while. A Siamese cat family had recently moved into a space beneath the pyracantha bushes behind my kitchen window. The mother had borne two litters. I'd counted eight kittens last time I'd looked. I peered out the window at them now: burrowing lumps. I went out back and left a bowl of water and two plastic plates of food for them.

I put a turkey pot pie in the oven and turned on the television. *Saloon Sluts* was playing on the cable access channel. It usually cycled back around every six months or so. As I ate I watched April's big death scene for maybe the seventh time. She was tied naked to stakes in the desert. I wondered what had become of her. Bombay Films had apparently shut down. The building next to the clinic sat empty these days.

I switched on the news. The Astros were still a pack of losers.

Well. There was no putting it off any longer. I set my crusty plate in the sink and called Paula. She was curt. She was *always* curt. "It's going to be tough this summer," she said. "I've got plans in July and August. I'm not sure when it will be possible for me to get the girls to you."

"What kind of plans?"

"Hawaii with my folks. Another trip with a friend."

"So I'll babysit the girls while you're gone."

"I want to take them with me. They're old enough now to appreciate travel."

"Paula, you need to make *me* part of your plans. They want to see me. Elissa said so just today."

"And I've been talking to Jimmy. I want to find a way to bring him into their lives on a more regular basis."

"A drive-by wave every ten years or so is not regular enough for you? I think that's what *he* has in mind."

"George! He's their father."

"Yeah. And where is he?"

"Where are *you*?"

"I'm right here, Paula. Where I've always been."

"Fuck you, George. You have no actual claim on us. Not the way Jimmy does."

"No? Ask the girls."

I heard them squealing in the background as she spoke. The circumstance—arguing with a woman while her children skittered around behind her—reminded me of how badly I'd blown it with Kelly. I'd had far more reason to stay connected to her than I did to Paula. But the tenderness I felt whenever I remembered Kelly was offset, always, by the knowledge of how poorly I'd treated Jean during that period. Then fate (or caprice or whatever) rolled into my lane on the freeway, overwhelming everything else in my life.

It was a losing game, weighing my various griefs.

With Paula, I didn't feel regret as much as generalized sadness that, in our respective desperation, we'd grabbed too swiftly for each other, leading to an inevitable disaster. Like Jean, Kelly had always displayed a refreshing directness. Not so Paula. She had a genius for dissembling. Still, even toward the end, when she wasn't talking to me much except to make excuses for not spending more time with me, sex with her remained urgent, blissful and absorbing. I gradually became aware that she was using sex to short-circuit my arguments, my criticisms, my dissatisfactions with our arrangements. Making love came to resemble a wrestling match. How reliable those damned old cliches proved to be!

It was a contest I wanted both to win and to lose right up to the day she called me a "stuffy old fart."

"Let's not fight, Paula," I said into the phone now. "I love the girls. And it's not just me they miss. They miss Houston. I think it's good for them to come here from time to time. Gives them a sense of continuity."

"*I'm* their continuity, George."

"Of course. But—"

"All right. Call me next week. I'll check the calendar again. We'll revisit this."

"Okay. Kiss them goodnight for me."

"Yeah."

Sleep was always impossible after Paula wound me up the way Paula could do. I put Son Seals on the hi fi and shut out the lights. I closed my eyes. I imagined myself in the bottomlands of the Mississippi River, sharing a bottle of rotgut with the ghost of Robert Johnson, learning to slide a pocketknife across the A string and hold it forever, a sweetly agonizing cricket vibrato.

As Son hummed above a snappy backbeat, moaning like a wronged old haint, I recalled Johnson's famous tale which every blues aficionado knows by heart: "If you want to learn how to play, you go to the crossroad. Be sure to get there little 'fore twelve at night. You got your guitar and be playin' a piece, sittin' there by yourself. A big Black man will walk up and take your box and he'll tune it. Then he'll play a piece and hand it back to you. That's how I learned to play anything I want."

And that's where *I* had decided to come back to life after Paula left. Right there, at Highway 61, where it hugged the gnarly, grassy border of US 49 (in the middle of the day, alas, with dozens of other tourists) I made a pact not with the devil but with myself.

"You can do anything you want," I said aloud as horseflies buzzed around me. I don't know why or how—willpower, I guess, a certain strength I thought I'd lost after the freeway accident—right there in the cradle of the blues the pounding misery of my life with Paula fell from me like a tossed-off winter coat. It was not long after that that I heard Spider at the Crackerbarrel Lounge.

In the dark in my apartment I surrendered to Son's Delta rhythms, rhythms quickened and honed by the steel and grit of Chicago, where so many blues players had drifted when heavy machines rolled in and ate up the South's dusky cotton. But not *all* of the South's players had drifted away, I thought, thinking of Spider.

On Friday I'd hear all about his Saturday show.

4.

Friday wasn't a teaching day for me. I spent the morning grading essays on the Battle of San Jacinto. The best paper, from one of my favorite students in the advanced class, concerned Santa Anna's life *after* he'd surrendered to Sam Houston. In his old age, the former general had been exiled from Mexico. He settled on Staten Island where he introduced chewing gum to North America. According to my student's sources, Santa Anna gave a hunk of chicle, the rubbery dried sap from sapodilla trees in southern Mexico, to an entrepreneur named Thomas Adams, who turned it into "Adams' New York Gum No, 1."

As I marked the paper, the fluorescent light above my desk fizzled and flickered. It was as though a small hand was opening and closing in front of it. I called maintenance. They said they couldn't get to it until late next week. I tried to keep working in the muted light but my concentration was shot. I'd been distracted all morning, anyway. I'd been thinking of calling Alice Richards and asking her to Spider's Juneteenth show.

Alice worked in the Affirmative Action Office. We'd dated a couple of times in the past two months and hit it off pretty well, though we'd never got beyond a goodnight kiss. I found her enormously attractive but she could be stiff. She was, I thought, overly zealous in pursuing her work: a thwarted crusader. She once told me about a sexual harassment case she'd overseen: "It's my job to be an advocate for the innocent, which on this campus—and in most other places, I assure you—are young women."

I didn't disagree but I suspected she often confused her advocacy with her own anger at men, the source of which I didn't know her well enough to trace. (But then, maybe most men assumed women who fought for sexual empowerment were angry at men. She *did* make me question my preconceptions, which suggested she *was* good at her job.)

"When I first came to Marion three years ago, I imagined no one could be nobler than people who teach in junior colleges," she said the night we first went out. "Clearly, they don't come here for the money, right? They'll never earn the prestige of their big-shot cousins in the major universities. They're just teachers. Servants of knowledge."

"And what've you learned since?" I asked.

"I've learned that pettiness, lust—all the nasties—are every bit as prevalent here as in the grand arenas. Maybe even more so since the perks in a place like this are so small." She gave a rueful laugh. We were dining at the Warwick, which advertised itself as the Southwest's "most rewarding hotel." It was nice but I'd always found it a little tacky. The bar was decorated with plush velvet chairs with tiny egg-shaped backs, gaudy golden chandeliers, smoky wall mirrors and copies of classical statues of nearly nude women. Houston's idea of Refined Taste.

The hotel was located near Rice University, where Jean used to teach, and Hermann Park. It was surrounded by long, beautiful rows of live oaks and cottonwoods. Limousines circled a tall, colorful fountain near its entrance. The Museum of Modern Art and the Contemporary Arts Museum were both just down the block. After show openings, Houston's culture-birds liked to be seen pouring champagne at the Warwick wearing strapless Halston gowns or Brooks Brothers suits. As Alice and I sipped wine in the piano bar after dinner, I overheard an exchange between a pair of transplanted New Yorkers. "I just adore living among the Texans," the first woman said. "They're such primitive sophisticates."

"What do you mean?" her friend asked.

"I mean they don't know what a blintz is. But if they did, darling, they'd love it."

I'd never felt at ease in this part of town except on the golf course at Hermann Park. It's where I'd first met Jean, chatting her up on the driving range. I was a terrible golfer and didn't play often—sometimes after class, now, on Monday afternoons I'd go hit a few. Hermann was a public course catering mostly to elderly Black men, retirees, and old-school newspapermen like Penrose who—by his lights—couldn't have chosen a more heavenly spot to croak in. The clubhouse served the best hamburgers in town.

The remaining area around the park—the hotel, the university, the med center, the elaborate brick homes—was too rich for my blood. But Alice had suggested the Warwick that night. She was right at home there.

I wasn't sure she'd be comfortable at the Juneteenth Festival. But *loosening her up* posed a sexy challenge. I loved to watch her cross her legs, to hear the hiss of her hose. Slow. In control.

The light above my desk quit altogether.

Apparently, Santa Anna never saw a profit from his gum. After being granted political amnesty he returned to Mexico. He died bitterly in poverty and neglect.

Sitting in the dark I punched Alice's number.

* * *

Every three hundred blocks or so the city's cigarette ads changed. In the Heights, the billboards showed a young white couple smoking and laughing on a sailboat. On Dowling Street, near downtown, a Black couple lay on a hill, smoking and laughing. In the barrios, Latino workers in a shower of welding sparks smoked and sweated and laughed.

"Black Magic here, tellin' you whitey up to no good—out to put our fine young men in chains! A hundred years or more we lived and sweated here in the heart of whitey's city and he still don't know us! Steal our music, steal our eats, even steal our party. Juneteenth, a holy day for our grandfolks, the day Texas slaves learnt they was free. Now the pigs want to shove in and steal a profit off our past, our prayers, our *good* times. Cain't even see us less we wearin' their fuckin' chains!" A burst of static nearly drowned him but then he came back strong. "Thurgood Marshall, James Nabrit, Barbara Jordan, Mickey Leland—*proud* Black history in the Bayou City. Don't let whitey tell you you invisible. What we gotta do? *Burn* his lies! Brothers, sisters, next time you see whitey sniffing round our hoods, our broken-hearted homes, you dog him, you bite him, you ride his moony ol' pig-ass. *You drive him the hell out!*"

Static finally swallowed him. I punched buttons until I found an R & B station: Junior Wells and "The Vietnam Blues." The tune featured a funny variation on the standard blues line. Instead of, "Woke up this mornin', found my baby gone," Junior sang, "Gonna wake up one mornin', find *yourself* gone."

I stopped by Spider's porch to hear about his show—really, to make sure he'd turn up. The young players in his band had come by in the morning to boost his confidence. He was feeling good again. He had his set list ready. "My tom-fills gonna set them booties on *fire!*"

"That's what I like to hear," I said.

I left him some smokes and said I'd be his biggest fan this weekend.

At home, I parked my car and walked around the apartment building to check on the kittens. The tiniest one was dead. I couldn't tell what had happened. Had it suffocated in the crush of its brothers and sisters as they'd snuggled for warmth at night? Or maybe its little lungs couldn't take the city's good intentions, the mosquito spray spread nightly by big white sanitation trucks.

I placed the kitten in a nearby dumpster, wrapping it in a napkin-nest next to some Chinese take-out boxes. The rest of the kittens seemed fine. Now that I'd started feeding them I felt responsible for them. I set two plates of Purina Cat Chow in a tangle of English ivy below the pyracantha bushes. Maybe there they'd be protected from predators.

On the sidewalk in front of the building, two teenage girls strolled past wearing cutoffs and white tank tops. They were discussing tattoos. "I just got a butterfly on my boob," one said. She had blond hair and chipped front teeth. "Looks like it's perching on my nipple."

"Did it hurt?" her friend asked.

"Hell yes, it hurt!"

Watching them, I felt delighted that the city worked at all when the odds were so clearly against it.

On the corner of Richmond, the girls bumped into the neighborhood bag lady, the one in the tumbleweed sweater. She'd come shuffling around a closed dry-cleaning store, blunt as a fullback. Even in ninety-degree heat she wore the sweater, an orange coat, galoshes, a thick wool cap and a pair of cotton gloves. Her skin was the same rough texture Pedro's had been, from long exposure to the elements. She carried half a dozen Dunkin' Donuts sacks stuffed with Colonel Sanders boxes. I'd seen her digging for fruit rinds or vegetable scraps in heaps of steaming trash. I hoped I'd buried the kitten deep enough in the dumpster.

When she collided with the girls she toppled backwards and lost control of her sacks. They scattered at her feet. The boxes popped open. Out spilled dozens of cicada shells, brittle husks *scritching* across the street.

The girls screamed, giggled and ran. The old woman tried to stand. I dropped my cat food bag, ran over and offered her a hand. "Are you all right?" I asked.

She squinted at me. "They have *all* our numbers," she grumbled. "Hold on to yours."

"I will," I said, uncomprehending. Sometimes I'd heard her in the mornings, before I was fully awake, shouting nonsense at the trees.

I helped her up.

A roach skittered across one of her sacks. "I own the goddam sky," she said. "Did you know I own the goddam sky?"

"You do a nice job with it," I said.

She grinned. Black gums, no teeth.

"Are you hungry?" I asked.

She smacked her dry, white lips. Crusts of skin trickled like toast crumbs from her mouth.

I gave her five dollars. "Get yourself a hamburger or something, okay?"

"You bet," she said. Her various garments smelled of rotten leaves. "You bet I will."

***

An Aztec god waving a spear against a pinched velvet background. A Lone Star ad. Purple piñatas swayed above sweating green bottles of beer sitting on a counter next to a March of Dimes jar. A young waitress snatched the bottles, shoved them onto a tray and danced across the room to a salsa beat pulsing from a flashing yellow jukebox.

The restaurant was only six blocks from my apartment but I hadn't been there in a while. I used to eat out every evening after Paula left. Tonight, when I'd checked my fridge after my run-in with the old woman on the street, I found only leftover chili (five days old—six?—it smelled like the old woman's boxes). I remembered Chimichanga.

The waitresses were all new, young and sexy in long, colorful skirts. The cook, a tough old hound named Carlos, recognized me. "Hey Professor! Long time no see!"

He used to kid me whenever I'd come in, order margaritas, and grade papers at one of the back tables: "Got homework tonight?"

I found my old spot. I pulled a pen and a pad of paper from my pocket. *Spider*, I wrote. *Roots?*

All afternoon, partly to settle my nerves about the weekend plans I'd made with Alice, I'd been figuring: one way to avoid exploiting Spider was to push beyond a pure academic reckoning of facts and dates; to tell the man's story fully, with dignity and respect, granting him perpetual life on the page. To do that, I'd have to know my subject much better than I did.

In one of our earliest conversations, Spider had told me, "My mama used to say we descended from slaves what come from the old Anansi tribe in Africa somewheres. Don't know much about 'em. They worshipped this god named Spider. Long arms, hairy ol' face. He's a storyteller, Mama said. Always remindin' people how they's made from the vines of the trees, the wretched mud of the earth. Stuff like that. Weavin' words like webs."

"Why did she tell you this? Do you remember?" I asked. "I mean, what was the occasion?"

"Mama say she named me for him. And it fits, I guess. 'Cause I'm a storyteller too, right, layin' down the news when I play, witnessin' for *my* people."

Spider called stories "go-alongs," "happenings" or "hoo-raws." I needed to know more about the blues' affinities with African storytelling traditions. *Anansi*, I wrote on my pad. Was the triple-beat rhythm so common in the tunes related to the natural syntax of Anansi speech? Drums—from the snare's high tones to the bellow of the tom-toms—had the power to mimic the full range of the human voice.

But more than African griot, I'd heard in Spider's "news" the chuffing of a plow through fertile Texas dirt, the shouts and melodic rags of field hands. Lullabies, spirituals, the cadences of longing—a centuries-old ache for escape, a mighty dash to freedom.

A waitress brought me a chili relleno and a cold Carta Blanca. At a table nearby, two Cajun men—I could tell they were Cajun from the stew of "hick" and French in their talk—argued about whether it was possible to go fly-fishing in the bayou. "Iss possible," one said. "But *stupide*. Nothin' but grass carp, catfish, red shiners—"

135

"Naw, main. Get you a good Wooly Bugger or a Royal Coachman, you be King of the Current."

I made some more notes while I ate. Spider was born on the Navasota River, northwest of Houston, an area still sumptuous with Cherokee and rich Spanish blood, the spilled blood of former slaves. Most whites and Blacks with Texas roots prior to 1880 had Native American ancestry. I pictured Spider's coppery, aqualine nose, his heavy brow.

It would be easy to dismiss him with a contemptuous glance if you just drove by him on the street: an old Black man lounging on his porch, sipping malt liquor in the middle of the day. But if you stopped and looked closely, you found yourself in the core of the Big Thicket, on the banks of the "Navasot" River, in the midst of a heady "go-along."

What seemed simple on the surface was a vital hodgepodge of Native tricksters and African gods (Papa Legba, guardian of the crossroads—did Robert Johnson know these tales? The god waited in the moonlight, demanding sacrifice from weary travelers); oral stories and coded drumbeats; field songs; electric guitars; country and city; money, sex, jukebox politics.

I sat back and sipped my beer, watched people come and go from the restaurant. Through its back door, which opened onto a small gravel parking lot, I saw a young Mexican in an apron light a cigarette for a woman wearing knee-high boots and a short blue skirt. Another aproned man carried a food tray across the lot to a small wooden shed out back. He knocked on the door. It opened just a crack. A needle of light sliced into the night from the shed and the man passed the tray inside.

I'd seen this before when I was more of a regular here. I'd always assumed illegals stayed in the shed, sleeping, eating, gathering strength before dispersing through the secret arteries of Houston then on to who-knows-where. Carlos seemed the type—like Kelly—who'd feed hungry people. Generous. Nonjudgmental. Faithful to his people.

The city had a million hidden "hoo-raws."

"How's your food, Professor?" Carlos called to me now, wiping his hands on a dishtowel the color of corn.

My mouth was full. I gave him a thumbs-up.

"'Nother beer?"

I nodded.

A trip to the Navasota River. Soon, I thought. Maybe I could even talk Spider into coming with me. He could show me the house where he was born, the backwoods juke joints he'd played as a kid.

The Cajuns rose and paid their tab. The taller of the two wore a yellow sport coat and bright red socks. His companion, a stubby man in a dark pullover sweater, plucked a toothpick from a plastic dispenser next to the cash register. On his way out, he accidentally bumped a table near the front door, spilling a pitcher of slushy margaritas. The trio at the table, two men and a woman, shouted in surprise. They jumped from their seats to avoid getting wet. The stubby man apologized. Carlos wiped the puddle with a rag. Before he was done, the trio was already laughing again, ordering more drinks.

I loved this place, its hominess, its ease. Worlds away from the Warwick. I couldn't picture Alice sitting here.

"Take it easy, Professor," Carlos said to me on my way out. The Aztec god shook his golden spear at the skies. I'd parked out back by the shed. As I unlocked my door, curtains rustled inside the shed's grimy window. Briefly I saw a child's dark forehead poke above the sill. A frightened glance. Then nothing.

***

Outside my apartment building, in the parking lot, I saw in the sweep of my headlights the bag lady angle headfirst into the dumpster. I stepped out of the car and locked it. "Hey!" I yelled.

She continued to dig.

"Hey! I put a dead animal in there! It's not healthy! Come out!"

She turned to look at me. A napkin, limp with catsup, stuck to an arm of her loosely-threaded sweater.

"What did you do with the money I gave you?"

She plucked the paper from her sleeve. She licked the catsup.

I pulled another five from my wallet. "Go eat. Please. They have burritos and popovers at the 7-Eleven down the street. Cold sandwiches."

She snatched the bill and leered at me.

Who the hell was she? How had she wound up here? In which feverish crease of Mama Houston's lap would she spend the night?

5.

I spent Saturday afternoon on a driving range near Hermann Park, hoping to exhaust my nervous energy before my date with Alice that night. Should I make a move? Ask her to stay over? I felt woefully out of practice, both the *asking* and the *doing*.

At the 270-yard marker, a man without a shirt steered a tiny John Deere tractor, snatching balls with a long metal pole and dropping them into a barrel on a cart attached to the tractor. For protection, he wore on his head a wire basket, the kind a dozen balls came in, which you paid for at the range entrance.

At the tee box next to me an old Black man cursed his driver. He'd just sent a polka-dotted ball past a dog in the field, well short of the tractor. "Die, motherfucker!" he hissed at his club.

The man on the tractor shooed the dog with the pole.

Jean had the most graceful swing of anyone I'd ever seen on a driving range. Thinking of Jean didn't help me prepare for Alice. I should have thought of that before coming here.

On a radio blaring from the clubhouse, a woman on a call-in show said, "About forty per cent of the money I spend in any given week, I spend unhappily."

The angry man snapped his driver on his knee.

I turned and left, knowing I'd not go back there again.

***

That night I took Alice to a little Chinese place on Richmond, not far from my apartment—nothing fancy but a tad more elegant than Chimichaga. Mr. Chen, the owner, knew only a few English phrases. "Hello. How are you? I think it is going to rain."

"Hi. We'll start with some egg rolls and a pot of green tea," I said.

"Very good. Thank you. Nice to see you."

Alice wore vanilla-colored slacks and a yellow blouse with red buttons. She'd pulled her hair back and tied it with a white ribbon. Simple. Gorgeous.

Mr. Chen returned with two tumblers of iced tea sprigged with mint leaves.

"Excuse me," I said. "We asked for the *hot* tea."

"Very good. It is certain to rain."

Alice wanted sweet-and-sour soup, Kung Pao chicken, stir-fried shrimp.

"Today we have pork only," said Mr. Chen. "Nice to see you. Enjoy your table forever."

I took a long time to unfold my napkin, making elaborate gestures, gearing up to ask Alice why an attractive woman like her was unattached. On our first couple of dates we'd avoided personal topics, talking instead about the college, the city.

"Oh, I was with a man for five-and-a-half years. It ended just last summer," she said. "He decided—discovered—he was gay." She laughed unconvincingly. "Ironic, right? Me, an Affirmative Action advocate, fiercely fighting sexual discrimination on all fronts . . . when he told me, I wanted to kill him and every gay man I could think of. For weeks, I had nightmares involving Elton John and a bloody ballpeen hammer. All to the tune of 'Rocket Man.'"

Mr. Chen set a steaming bowl of pork and bamboo shoots on our table. "Nice to see you," he said.

Goldfish swam in a big blue tank by the door. They looked like wontons floating in a meager soup. Four fine-suited men arrived and requested the best table by a window overlooking the street.

The pork smelled like peppermint.

"So now I guess you're mad at *all* men," I said, trying to sound jokey.

"No, I don't hate men," Alice said, quite serious. "I just don't like them very much."

We spent the rest of the meal in near-silence. Afterward, I drove us downtown. A plastic Budweiser bottle, tall as a grain silo, fastened by guy wires to the ground, towered over Emancipation Park near the corner of Wheeler and Dowling. Radio stations gave away T-shirts, posters, cassette tapes.

I bought us two cold cups of beer at a concession stand. Alice stiffened, watching the crowd. She stood close to me. "Dowling Street was named for an Irish barkeep—Dick Dowling—who helped the Confederate army win the battle of Sabine Pass," I explained, fresh out of small talk and afraid to get too intimate. "He lured a bunch of Yankee boats into a nasty port, knowing they'd run aground on an oyster reef." This was the kind of tale that made Paula call me a "stuffy old fart."

Alice said the story was *very* interesting. She'd even claimed to like Mr. Chen's. She smiled and raised her cup to mine. Apparently, she was more game than I thought.

She'd come from Eugene, Oregon and had only lived in Texas for a couple of years. "I'm having a little trouble with this 'Juneteenth' thing," she said. "*What's* it about?"

"Well, Lincoln signed the Emancipation Proclamation on January 1, 1863, right?"

"If you say so."

"But it wasn't until June 19, two years later, when a Union general defeated Rebel holdouts in Galveston, that slaves here in Texas—about 300,000 of them—learned the truth."

"All that time? They were free and didn't know it?"

"Yep. After that, for over a hundred years, families here celebrated the day informally. In '79 it became an official Texas holiday."

"Hm."

"Something wrong? You haven't touched your beer."

Instead of answering right away she stared at a man who'd bumped past us sucking a flask of MD 20/20. The back of his T-shirt said "Black by Popular Demand." He raised his flask and shouted, "Hallelujah!" A pretty young girl with twin baby girls in her arms danced to the beat of her Walkman.

"It's awful to admit this because it's part of my job to protect civil rights and stuff," Alice whispered now. "But I've never been around this many Black people. In Oregon, you know, there just aren't that many—"

"You're scared?"

"A little. Yeah. I confess."

Maybe five hundred people had come to see the fireworks and to listen to the blues, only a handful of whom were white. "There's no need to be frightened," I said. "This is a night of joy."

"You've done this before?"

"Juneteenth? Sure. Come on. Let me introduce you to my friend Spider."

We cut through a gap in an orange mesh fence to reach the backstage platform. Graffiti curled across a picnic table next to a bank of lights: "We are one world of tempted humanity." "Shit," "Piss," "Fuck."

Spider was perched on a metal garbage can beside an ice chest, guzzling a Lone Star longneck. He wore a straw fedora, shades and a light pink cotton shirt. He'd jammed a pair of drumsticks into his back jeans pocket.

At his feet lay a wrinkled newspaper. Water, beer and mud had smudged the headlines: "Pentagon Officials Say . . . apes."

"Looking good," I said.

Spider raised his arm. "Feel like a bar of iron, man."

"Shake it off. Just nail down the beat." I offered him a Camel. "This is my friend Alice."

"Say baby, what up?"

She blushed.

"Can't wait to hear you. We'll be out front," I said.

"Break a leg," Alice ventured.

"Mm-hmm." Spider looked her up and down, staring hard at her calves.

Alice brought a hand to her throat and abruptly walked away.

"What I say?" Spider said. "*Sen*-si-tive. She royalty or somethin'?"

"It's all right," I said. "Good luck, man." I ran to catch Alice. "Hey."

"I know, I know. I know what you're going to say. Relax, right? This isn't the college."

"Alice, he didn't mean anything by it."

"It's just a good-time party. Sexual harassment isn't sexual harassment here."

"I'm sorry. That's just Spider."

"And by the way, George, they *never* mean anything by it."

"Okay. One song? And then we can go if you like."

She took a breath. "No. No, I don't mind staying. It's just . . . I'm a little nervous, like I said."

We wove through the crowd, staying near the stage. After a minute or two, I noticed four men following us closely. They wore baggy shorts and LA Lakers shirts. It seemed that Alice's fears were contagious.

She turned to me. "Do you ever worry that you're barging into a world that isn't really yours?"

"I worry about it all the time."

"How do you reconcile it to yourself?"

"Respect," I said. "I just try to treat everybody with respect." She nodded.

We found a cool, dry spot about fifteen feet from the amplifiers. I took off my windbreaker and spread it on the ground for Alice. A radio DJ—I recognized the voice but not the man—took the stage in front of Spider's sparkling black drums. "Freedom!"

he shouted. The crowd chanted "Freedom!" right back at him. "Friends, we're here tonight to remind ourselves how steadfast and resilient is the African-American heart! For centuries, it has endured untold indignities—"

"Tell it!"

"—tragedies—"

"Say it, brother!"

"—shame—"

"Amen!"

"—and emerged triumphant!"

A jubilant chorus. Alice reached for my hand.

"We must never forget: the price of Liberty is eternal vigilance!"

Applause like small-arms fire, rapid and distinct.

"Now. You ready for some blues?"

"Bring it!"

"Welcome back, then, a Houston legend: Spider Lammamoor!"

Spider stepped from the wings, tipping his hat. He raised his beer in a triumphant communal salute.

The bass player began a three-chord stutter-step. Spider followed with a kickbeat. His arms and legs snapped crisply through syncopated bends and slides, through gospel and blues, rockabilly chit-chat and streaming, old-time swing. He walked the bass down double-stops and burning, bold glissandos: Look here, like that, ah-*ha*!

The smells of barbecued chicken and buttery corn on the cob mingled with the sizzle of hot dogs in the city's humid air.

> I carried my baby to the doctor this mornin'
> This is what he said
> He said, You better be careful with this woman
> Man, she almos' dead

The grass smelled of standing rainwater and fertile roots, webby leaves.

I jus' want my woman to be happy here
Happy wherever in this world she go.

The young men in Lakers attire edged forward, right behind a family next to me. I tightened my grip on Alice's hand.

Spider swung the band into a pseudo-waltz with a ragged gospel top. He pulled a mike over his ride cymbal and moaned into it, "Shoo-fly in a windstorm . . . "

I laughed. I'd given him the line. Preparing for class one day, I'd been reading WPA-era slave narratives and come upon the story of Jeremiah Harris, an ex-slave. He said fighting slavery was "like a shoo-fly in a windstorm. People so tiny and the man so huge." I'd repeated those words to Spider on his porch one morning.

"Shoo, shoo, shoo-fly . . . "

Between the first and second sets I led Alice backstage again. I knew she was ready to go. Spider was back on the trash can, reminiscing about his old buddies: Nathan Abshire, Big Maceo, One-Hand Sam. The younger musicians listened intently. "Sam be pickin' with his right hand, spoonin' down that snap-bean gumbo with his left. Good Condition Boy, Sam. Drunk hisself to deaf right here on Dowling Street. Couldn't make him live, no matter what we done."

I gave him a hug. "Didn't I tell you, man, the blues is alive and well? You sounded great."

"Feelin' purty good." He popped the cap on a longneck. "Gotta thank you, George. Talkin' me back into this hoo-doo."

"It's where you belong."

"The songs were very nice," Alice mumbled, teetering close to me. "Thank you for the show."

"Any time, Missy."

I felt her shiver but she smiled. She told me the amplifiers had given her a slight headache, she was enjoying herself, really she was, but could we possibly—

"Of course." I squeezed Spider's arm. "Gotta run," I said.

"Yeah, I see."

"Drop by Monday?"

"Bring me some smokes, awright?"

I walked Alice back through the park past the giant plastic beer bottle, the hot dog stands, mothers and fathers and children, cotton candy. On the street, kids ran in packs of four or five past parked cars, excited by the music. No breeze. The air was hot. Crickets echoed the beat of the songs. A television flickered through someone's rusty screen door—an old Western. A tricycle lay on its side in the yard.

Fireworks burst above dry oaks. Alice looked up. The explosions above us shaded her face pink then yellow and green. I realized again how beautiful she was but . . . *she didn't like men very much*. Her beauty demanded something of me. What was it?

I unlocked the car. As Alice was about to step inside, brakes squealed in the street. Over the grinding insistence of a hip-hop tune a voice called, "What you *wont* here, white boy?"

I turned to see the Lakers—four of them—hanging out the windows of a sleek white Mustang. It was the cruiser from Spider's neighborhood.

"Motherfucker confused. He think he a *brother*, Deke."

I was glad I no longer had the Chrysler tricked-up as a low rider.

Alice looked at me, ashen. I remembered I'd stored my golf clubs in the trunk. A four-wood might be handy . . .

"It just like Black Magic say. Comin' down here, listen *our* music, eat *our* food, dance *our* gig."

Right. Right. I'd been driving around appreciating Black Magic without really listening to what he said.

"On'iest thing he couldn't do, Deke, was find him some Black pussy so he stuck with *that* piece of shit!" The boys laughed.

Gently, I nudged Alice into the car and locked her door. I arranged my keys into spikes between my fingers and walked slowly around to the driver's side. The Mustang idled right behind us. *Respect*, I thought. "We're just leaving, "I said.

146

"Damn straight, motherfucker."

The one called Deke dropped a malt liquor bottle onto the pavement. It shattered with an ugly pop.

"George," Alice whispered when I slipped behind the wheel. "George, what do we do?"

"It's all right." I turned the key and inched cautiously away from the curb. The Mustang followed. Another malt liquor bottle sailed into the street ahead of my car. I swerved to miss flying shards. In my rear-view I saw cigarettes flare behind the cruiser's tinted windows.

Among barking horns, beneath flashing yellow fireworks, I twisted down backstreets in Black neighborhoods, past a largely Latino block, through intersections where the city's old grid pattern ducked beneath the new. Garbage pails. Billboards. The rattling drone of air-conditioners pushed beyond their capacities.

Shoo-fly in a windstorm.

In a Trinidadian barrio in the northwest part of town a small Juneteenth celebration was just getting underway. Salsa music kicked out of two giant stereo speakers in the back of a Dodge pickup. Twenty or thirty girls danced in the street, sweating and sexy, wearing black and yellow Danskins, ankle bracelets and wobbly sombreros shaped like broken umbrellas.

I seemed to have lost the Lakers, at least temporarily. "Tell you what we'll do," I told Alice. "We'll park the car here, tucked away on this little street between these trucks. We'll lose ourselves in the crowd for half an hour."

She looked around. "You're sure *this* neighborhood is safe?"

"Don't worry."

Confetti sprinkled the air. Children wrapped themselves in streamers. A tall, copper-colored woman beat her buttocks with a bottle as she danced to the music from the pickup. Nearly nude kids skipped around a laughing man stretched like a corpse in a giant cardboard box.

I kept a careful watch and explained to Alice that, under British rule, generations of Trinidadians had been forced into slavery in

147

the cane fields or on large sugar plantations. At carnival time, they carried whips and chains and painted their faces with flour to parody their white masters: "A play-revolution to head off the real one."

"Yeah, but the real ones are still just a heartbeat away, aren't they?"

"I'm sorry, Alice. I had no idea we'd run into trouble. It's just a handful of folks who can't get beyond—"

"You go along, thinking everything's fine, the country's getting better—"

"Would you like another beer?"

Behind her, a young man in a Ronald Reagan mask bounced on a car hood. His shirt said "Suck My Dick." A woman sashayed past me wearing a hula skirt and a cowboy hat. "Happy June-teenth," she said and patted my ass.

Alice was on the verge of tears.

I don't know why, beyond attraction—or as an apology for exposing her to danger—but I leaned over and kissed her lightly on the lips. Maybe it was a preemptive strike against the moral lesson I felt certain she was about to deliver.

She looked startled. She blushed. Then she smiled.

"Am I over the line?" I asked.

"I don't know. Are you?"

"Maybe we should—"

"Yes."

We walked back to the car. She held my hand. Suddenly, we were as shy as schoolkids. A Roman candle split a wall of smoke in the sky. Its light illuminated an old man pawing through a dumpster. I remembered I'd forgotten to feed the kittens.

No sign of the Mustang. I drove past the junior college, over to Montrose. In front of my place I killed the engine and shut off the lights. A water sprinkler *chrred* in the dark. Someone's dog barked.

"Alice, I'm—"

"Shhh."

Her mouth was more expressive than Paula's, pressing and tentative all at once, exploring and waiting to be explored. Imagine if she *liked* men!

"Do you want to come in?"

She nodded.

The air in my apartment was dusty and stale. I opened a kitchen window and switched on a ceiling fan. "Wine?"

"Just a touch."

An uncorked bottle of chardonnay sat in the fridge next to three soggy half-cut lemons and a plate of leftovers. Broccoli-cheese casserole. The Cling Wrap was loose around the dish. It smelled like a swamp. "Whoa," I said, stepping back. "Sorry. Living alone, you know . . . " I scraped the food into a trash bag then set the plate in the sink, too hard. It chipped. Alice just watched me.

I handed her a glass of wine and pulled her gently down the hall. In my bedroom I opened another window. I set our glasses on a night table and unbuttoned her blouse. The V of her collarbone moved sleekly inside her flesh. Angles veered surprisingly into soft places, pockets of heat into which my hands fit, just so.

As we moved together, my body felt less like my own than like an extension of hers, fluttering, charged by our motion.

Wind chimes sang from a neighbor's yard through the open window. Then another sound. Wailing. Alice stopped. "What's that?" she said.

I sat up. "Oh." I rubbed my face. "It's a street lady. Poor thing. She hangs around the dumpsters and talks to herself. I'll close the window."

"No. No, stay here." She tightened her grip on my back and buried her face in my shoulder. The gesture brought tears to my eyes.

Beside her head, wobbling on the night table next to the wine glasses, I noticed the glass skunk Jean had given me years ago in Galveston. We'd gone crabbing that Saturday morning, using chicken necks as bait to entice the crabs. The creatures scrambled over green and purple pebbles onto blistering sand and into Jean's net. I'd seen the skunk in a gift shop on the Strand. It made me laugh: its big eyes and its pompadour. Jean bought it for me when I wasn't looking and surprised me with it later in our beachside motel room. That night, the skunk danced on the bed's headboard while we made love, a salty breeze riffling the gold curtains around our sliding glass door, the crabs clattering in a plastic bucket in the bathtub, crammed with chipped, dirty ice . . .

My tears came harder now. Alice looked up at me. All the meaningless little moments Jean and I had shared together—the way she'd cried when she'd found a dead blue jay in the yard one steamy August night; her delight when she'd first tasted cilantro at a picnic, just the two of us, on a baseball diamond near Rice; my laughter when I'd spotted the skunk in the shop. Only I was left to remember them now.

Alice dabbed my cheeks with her fingertips. She smiled. "It's all right," she said. "It's all right."

6.

My best moves were father-moves: ice cream treats in the middle of the day, an unexpected raise in the girls' weekly allowance. Granting or withholding praise, depending on the girls' achievements. Once, when Elissa had managed all As in school my praise had been extravagant. The day Jane shaved the hind legs of a neighbor's schnauzer with her mother's electric razor—an impressive achievement, no matter how you viewed it—I thought it best to hide my pride in her ingenuity.

I was my finest self with the girls, just as I had been, I thought, with Monica and Kate, years earlier. I knew how much I'd miss them when Paula left but I didn't know how many changes I'd miss in short bursts. They'd leave me at the end of August after Paula had agreed to a summer visit; by December, in photos accompanying their Christmas cards, they'd be different creatures altogether. One loose tooth had turned into a gaping chasm in a mouth. Throbbing joints had stretched into an extra half-inch of height.

I couldn't even imagine Monica and Kate now.

Who would Elissa and Jane be *this* summer?

I punched Paula's number. 9:30 Sunday morning: my regular time to speak to the girls. At around dawn Alice had asked me to take her home. I had hoped for a leisurely breakfast with her. She swore she'd had a good time, no regrets, but she had a lot to do before work on Monday . . . yes, yes, of course I could call her. Confused, self-conscious after sex, shocked by my apartment in the daylight—something. Her stiffness had returned. Unable to kid her out of it, I didn't try to talk her into staying.

Now Jane was saying into the phone, "George, I'm going to be in a play at school."

"That's great, Janie. Is it a singing play?"

"No."

"Is it a dress-up play?"

"George. *All* plays are dress-up plays."

"I guess so."

Elissa had learned to play "chest."

"Chest?"

"You know. Kings and queens and pawns."

"Ah. How'd you learn to play?"

"I *know* how to play, George."

"But did someone teach you to—"

"I just *know*, okay?

"Okay, darling."

I made no headway with Paula regarding a summer visit with the girls. I felt frustrated and lonely after hanging up the phone. I thought of calling Alice but that would make me seem desperate and pathetic. *Was* I desperate and pathetic?

At Weingarten's I bought a *New York Times* and some orange juice. I went home and made myself scrambled eggs. I spread the fat paper on my table. Critics said that if George W. Bush was elected in the fall he'd find some excuse to invade Iraq. Bush's supporters dismissed such talk. Iraq was a bad actor, they said, but Bush was a pragmatist (a good, solid Texan) and containment would continue to be US policy. Meanwhile, Assistant Attorney General Lanny Breuer was celebrating El Salvador's amendment of its constitution, allowing for extradition to the United States. The change signaled success in "our continuing efforts to work with our partners around the world to make sure criminals cannot find safe haven from justice," Breuer said. Given the US's covert activities in Central America over the last two decades, and its criminalization of immigrants fleeing wars the US had helped escalate, I figured this new development was a means of establishing political cover for continued US meddling. I could just imagine Kelly's reaction, down in Arizona.

An article in "Living Arts" said that Memphis Minnie, an early blues singer "whose howling, rhythmic calls rose out of the gritty Mississippi Delta cotton fields in the 1920s" had finally gotten a grave marker in the cemetery at New Hope Baptist Church in Walls, Mississippi just off Highway 61. When she'd died in '72, the "music industry had passed her by, as had any profits from her work," the paper said. She'd been laid in a pauper's grave. Now a handful of blues fans—all white—had established a memorial fund to recognize several long-forgotten Southern musicians.

I wondered, briefly, if I could give the girls a tour of the Delta in August. Paula wouldn't allow it but maybe she wouldn't have to know. Could the girls keep such a secret? Probably not.

Below my open kitchen window the kittens romped under bushes. I heard scrabbling and loud purring. I was nearly out of cat food. Except for grading the test I'd given on Thursday—and I could already tell that half the class had tanked—I had the day free. I figured now might be a good time to check out the animal shelter I'd seen last summer when I'd taken the girls to Hobby Airport for their flight back to New Orleans. Recently, I'd remembered the shelter and wondered if it might be wise to take the kittens there so the place could find proper homes for them.

I did the dishes—*clean*, for Alice's next visit!—then drove out Curry Road. Porno shops, massage parlors, gun stores . . . I'd always hated this part of town, the rent-by-month apartments for cut-rate merchants moving God-knows-what through the Hobby terminal. It always depressed me, driving the girls out here to return them to their mother. The neighborhoods reeked of the middle man—the buildings, bland and cheap, as temporary and indifferent as their occupants. Fast food, fast lives, instant entertainment needing no skills. On Curry Road, on the grassy median, a large brown dog lay dead. I turned, past a "Five-Minute Wedding Chapel" next to "Nelda's Super-Hair." A "Militia Supplies" shop anchored a commercial strip next to a liquor store and three cramped pawnshops. Pickups displaying Confederate flag stickers circled the lot.

At a gravelly intersection I saw a faded wooden sign. I couldn't remember exactly but I thought the sign might mark the path to the shelter. I turned. Sweat stung my eyes. The air smelled of pine and of tar from the streets. I braked hard. The road had abruptly ended. Grit flooded the car through my window.

In a weedy field in front of me a bulldozer bashed the roof of a car. The operator tugged the levers, raising the shovel's arm then brought the arm crashing down on a brown and white Toyota. The car lurched. Glass exploded from its windshield. No one was around.

Who was this idiot? A city worker? Why was he destroying an automobile in a deserted neighborhood on the hottest day of the summer? I wanted to scream about the senselessness of it. I leaned out the window and saw in my side mirror a bright white building behind me. It was shaped a little like the Astrodome, only much smaller.

I kicked my car into reverse. Umbrellas of dust rose from the rear wheels. The bulldozer readied for another punch.

A small sign above the building's door said "Forever Friends: Animal Shelter."

It smelled like a hospital—not antiseptic exactly; medicinal, riddled with sickness. Wet fur, foul breath. Something else. I sniffed deeply. Of course. Gas. Just a trace of it. Immediately, I knew that coming here had been a mistake. I couldn't possibly trust this place with the kittens.

A young woman at the front desk was reading a profile of the Bush family in the *Houston Chronicle*. She looked up and asked if she could help me. I lied and said I was searching for a lost cat. She said I could check the back cages. The shelter kept animals for two weeks before "we have to put them to sleep."

She led me to a massive metal door with a square glass pane in its center. When she tugged the handle a gust of heat emerged from the hall. I thanked her and stepped into the suffocating broil.

Floor-to-ceiling black wire cages lined either side of the room. Deep runnels gouged the red-painted floor. A clear liquid ran through the grooves. It smelled like pesticide.

Barking, wailing—the sounds deafened me. An emaciated German shepherd rushed the walls of its cage, gnashing its teeth at me. I stumbled against the opposite wall and felt hot breath on my ankles: two toy poodles snapped at my heels. Frayed red ribbons dangled, dirty, from their necks. A large yellow dog lay in a cage by itself. It lifted its head, a rheumy old man.

By the far wall, cats swarmed together in cages: a noisy spin-cycle of motion. Too many "hoo-raws" in the city, even among the animals. I couldn't help but think, *This is where the city's discarded creatures come to die.* I hurried out of the room, muttering vague excuses to the woman at the desk.

Outside, the bulldozer knocked the Toyota's trunk lid off its hinges.

***

Rap music rattled Dowling Street's brightly lit projects. Streamers and paper cups littered the streets from yesterday's celebration. Spider was perched on his stoop sipping "juice" from a jam jar.

I killed my engine and called from the curb, "Join you?"

"Sure."

"Great show yesterday."

"Thank you. Didn't 'spect you till tomorrow. What brings you? Bad news? Usually bad news brings a fella round when no one's 'spectin' him."

155

"No, not really. Nothing terrible, anyway. I'm just a little unsettled."

"Hell, I been *unsettled* since slidin' out my mama's womb." He handed me the wine bottle. "I get you a glass."

Crickets wheedled in the grass. From a dim window above Spider's porch a smell of gin and barbecued chicken tumbled over me. Down the block, where the shackled Black hands peeled on the rough brick wall, a broken police tape fluttered like kite string from a tree.

"Had a drive-by earlier today," Spider explained. "Twelve-year-old boy nicked in the arm."

I looked around for the Mustang.

Spider shook his head. "Why someone want to eighty-six a twelve-year-old boy?"

"You know, last night, some fellows chased me away from the park."

Spider raised an eyebrow.

"Seems to be a high degree of . . . *territoriality* around here," I said.

"Brothers protecting they turf? Yeah. Black Magic's got 'em all riled up."

"Who is he?"

"Who is he really, I don't know. Just some brother with a microphone. But he a guardian angel to some folks. Anyways, George, anyways, I'm feelin' good 'bout the weekend. Obliged to you for nudgin' me back onstage. "

"I loved 'Shoo-fly.'"

"Standard blues juke. Nothin' much. C to C sharp."

"With a 2/4 bar?"

"You learnin'! Ride cymbal keepin' the beat, leavin' the bass drum free to bust some chops. Let me ast you, man. Somethin' you tol' me while ago. *Slaves* used to live here? On Dowling Street. Tha's on the level?"

"Right here." I poured more wine. It tasted like lighter fluid.

"Reason I ast, sometimes I think I can hear 'em. You know? In my head, in the music. Them old chains jukin' back and forth, like they won't let go."

"You said it. You're a storyteller," I said. "Sometimes I think telling stories . . . it's like carrying people's spirits around inside you."

"Yeah."

I thought of Pedro, the Thuots and the Zamoras. The women at the Casa. People come and go . . . and only the stories remain.

"Those old spirits, Spider. It's something I wanted to talk to you about. You know what I'd like to do? I'd like to see where you were born. See the first joints you played."

"In the Thicket, you mean?"

"Yeah. I've been thinking it'd be great if I could write *your* story—because it parallels the music's path, from rural to urban, right, from the cotton fields to the backroom speakeasies."

"Let me tell you, I don't think you should go there, man. Not on your own. Back in them woods it's still . . . *territorial*, okay?"

"Would you take me?"

"Hm. When you want to go?"

"Anytime. Now. This week."

"Shit! Man on *fire!*"

"We could just take a day, maybe two . . . "

"Tell me. This *unsettlement* you feelin? It have somethin' to do with Little Miss Ann you brung to the Juneteenth party?"

"No. Well . . . a little. And there's some other stuff. I'd just like to get away. Turn my mind to something else."

"Turn your ass to gettin' *killed*, you go stompin' round some of them hollers in the Thicket," he said. "Thing is, since Sat'day we had offers to play most ever' night. Mr. Gino's Lounge. The Club Success. Etta's. C. Davis Bar-B-Q. And the beauty part is, these *Black* joints. The real thing. No white slummin' goin' on."

"That's great. Okay. So . . . if I happen to go poking around those woods and I come back with questions, you'll answer them for me?"

"You bring me some smokes."

"Deal."

"Meantime, George, you better get straight wit' your womens," Spider said. "And *watch* your skinny ass."

7.

On Monday my students were noisy, eager to see their test grades, secretly thrilled (like a herd of wild ponies) by the threatening weather outside. The classroom was muggy. It smelled of chalk and damp cotton clothing. I set the test folder on the seminar table. A quarter of the class had failed. Basic world history.

I returned the exams. Somberly, the students read their results. The Asians rolled their eyes, some with pleasure, others with disappointment. The Latinos straightened vainly or sank. The Arabs revealed nothing.

Thunder slammed the building's thin walls.

I hadn't used my world map exercise with this particular class. There hadn't been time—the summer term was short. I could tell they weren't in a receptive frame of mind. If I drilled them again over the test material, most of them wouldn't retain it any better than they had the first time around, and the rest would be bored. "All right, everyone, put your tests away. We'll talk about it next time. In the meantime, I want you to get out a blank sheet of paper and draw me a world map. Quickly, now! Don't even think about it."

Some of the students gave me squirrely looks but they reached for their pens. A few of them worked with fluency and joy. Most seemed to fight their simple tools.

When they finished, and I asked them to compare their efforts, they were astonished—as I knew they would be—at the differences in their drawings.

Africa front and center.

Over here, Saudi Arabia at the core.

On one map, Lima, Peru was the earth's navel.

"So," I said. "Will the real world please stand up?"

They didn't understand me.

"What does this teach us?" I asked.

They all agreed that a person's image of the planet depended on where they came from.

"Our home cultures, our national and regional biases, blind us to others' conceptions of the truth," I said. "And we all have individual biases as well. Most of us can't see our culture—the basic set of assumptions shaping our strongest beliefs—any more than a fish can see the bowl it's swimming in."

"My teacher." Karim, a young Tunisian, waved his hand. "I think maybe it means something more."

Karim was one of my best students, naturally friendly and charming.

"I think maybe it means . . ." He worked his mouth around the innate clumsiness of words. "The world? She is, perhaps, unknowable."

***

In my office after class I tried to phone Alice but her secretary said she'd called in sick this morning. I tried to reach her at home but her machine picked up. "I hope you're okay," I said. "Please call me. I'd like to see you again. Next time, we'll find a *safe* part of town. Promise."

The overhead light flickered and went out.

I punched Paula's number, hoping to talk to the girls. Of course they were in day school—I wasn't thinking—and I got into an argument with Paula. "You talked to them yesterday, George. *Sunday* is your day."

"Can't I just call them whenever I want?"

"Why?"

"*Why?* You have to ask me why?"

"I'd rather not ask you anything at all, George."

"Fine!"

I hung up and stared, in the semi-dark, at another stack of papers waiting to be graded. I couldn't face them. I couldn't face *anything*, just then. Especially my suspicion that I'd pissed Alice off. Or traumatized her. I called and left a message with the dean's secretary. "I have some personal business and I'll be gone the next two days. Could you post notices on my classroom doors? My students have their assignments."

I drove to my apartment, packed a toothbrush and a change of clothes. I left two plates of cat food in the bushes.

***

Virgin of Guadalupe candles washed Chimichanga in thick, eggy light. I'd intended to place a to-go order, take the food with me and eat it on the road. But the place was so warm— *somnambulant*—I decided to linger a while before setting out.

I dipped a tortilla chip into a *mulcahete* brimming with thick green salsa. I watched cooks step furtively through the restaurant's back door carrying trays of steaming beans and rice. Through a window lined with tiny white light bulbs (shaped like laughing skulls) I saw the cooks cross the parking lot balancing the trays and tap on the door of the shed.

Places like this, dozens of them—hundreds?—must have replaced the Casa, years ago, when the cops shut it down.

A baleful waltz poured from the jukebox speakers.

I tried Alice's number from a pay phone by the bathrooms. No answer. As I stood there, I overheard a cook trundle through the plastic-bead curtain in the kitchen doorway, just around the corner. He told Carlos, "New group tonight."

"How many?"

"Two families."

"From?"

"Michoacán."

"We clear enough room?"

"I sent Billy to K-Mart for three more sleeping bags."

I heard the cook leave. The beads clicked like spitting rain. I stepped around the corner. "Carlos?" I said.

He leaned through the curtain. "Professor! What can I do you for? How's your food?"

"Fine. Listen, can I ask you something?"

"Oh my. Sounds serious." He smiled, his skin squeezing the dimple in his chin and revealing big yellow teeth.

"I don't mean to pry into your business but . . . the shed out back? The trays?"

"What trays?"

"I'm sorry . . . it's just . . . if you're feeding people back there—"

Carlos shook his head.

"The thing is, there's a homeless woman in my neighborhood, near here. She sleeps behind a dumpster. I give her money for food but she doesn't eat well. She's a little funny in the head. If you've got a . . . I don't know . . . a system going here, I wondered if you could possibly make room for one more every so often . . . "

He stared at me hard. Behind me, flamenco guitar from the jukebox. Glass-scrapes. A hissing of steam from the kitchen.

Carlos squeezed my arm. He looked me in the eye. I thought he was going to throw me out but instead he pulled me around the corner, into shadow. "Do you think you could get her to come around after dark? On Tuesdays or Wednesdays?" he said.

"I'll try."

He looked around. "I deny everything, of course."

"Yes. Of course. Me too."

"I just remember where I came from, is all. This woman. She from here?"

"I don't know."

162

"Well. Maybe a little rice and beans. We'll see, Professor."

"Thank you, Carlos."

He shook his head. "It's no way to run a business."

"I mean it. Thank you."

***

"Pigs be comin' for me, folks, so we on the move tonight, somewheres in the city. Smoked me outta my house. You be next, brothers. Bastards won't rest till they steal all the Black property in town. Mark me. Sendin' dope and guns into our 'hoods, scarin' up reasons to invade."

I fiddled with the fine-tune, hoping for a stronger signal.

"They right behind me, brothers. You hear that? Yessiree. Si-*reens*." He laughed. "Pig squeals. Whole passel of 'em. I'm broadcastin' now on foot. They bustin' down doors, grabbin' up women and children, astin' 'bout *me*. Wanna shut down the truth. But I ain't goin.'"

A car backfired on the freeway ahead of me. I jumped.

Now there was only silence where Black Magic had just been screaming defiance. The fine-tune did nothing except increase the levels of static. My skin went cold.

I used to tell Monica and Kate, as well as Elissa and Jane, that if they ever saw a scary shadow on the wall at night and couldn't sleep, they shouldn't hide beneath the covers. Stare at that silly shadow, I said. Study it. Walk right up to it until you see it's nothing to fear.

George, are we coming to see you?

I set my cruise control on 65 and headed for the Thicket.

8.

It could have been Mississippi in 1930, the rich, alluvial furrows of the Delta where Robert Johnson met the Devil and the roots of the blues grew wild. But this was Texas just after century's end.

Algier Alexander bellowing his fierce field-hollers, his prison and farm labor laments; Blind Willie Johnson slurring hellfire, scraping a pocketknife across rain-rusted strings; Black Ace, Mance Lipscomb slinging echoes of vaquero guitar—it was high time I came here to sample their fertile soil.

Around one a.m. I stopped at the Trail's End Motel in Paley, the only place open for miles. The old woman at the registration desk had a face like a washrag stiffened with layers of dried soap. She gummed a Winston beneath a crackling yellow light. "We'll go for days, weeks, even months here 'thout seeing someone from the city," she said.

"That right?" I signed my name and license plate number on an index card.

In my room, by the dim light of a lamp scarred with cigarette burns and the blue pulsing of a soft-porn movie on TV—the one clear channel—I re-read my transcripts of interviews with Spider, memorizing place-names and directions so I could find landmarks and key spots tomorrow. In the room next to mine, a woman sang, "Hey hey, we're the Monkees."

I made notes on Houston's Black protests—*upsets*, Spider called them. The race riot of 1917, when Black soldiers from Camp Logan, a military outpost in the city, marched through white subdivisions firing their rifles, enflamed by racist police. The "Dowling Street Shootout" in the 1970s, when cops killed the leader of a Black militant group called the People's Party II, sparking violence and looting.

These incidents must have been mythologized in neighborhood songs. If so, were they set to familiar melodies passed from one generation to another? Could I find a direct connection between music from the Thicket and recent urban verses?

The next morning, armed with my notes, I set out. My car was the only one in the lot. The sky was velvet green patched with purple clouds. The ground smelled rank and moist.

"Friends, the Devil owns several hundred acres here in southeast Texas. He's the biggest *jefe* in these-here parts. If he offers you any property—a pretty riverside casita, a rose garden—take my word for it, walk away. Don't be tempted to buy. No sir. The mortgage is more than you can afford."

I switched the radio off, still mourning Black Magic's absence. The sky grew stranger, as though a child had shaded it wrong in a coloring book. Wind jiggled the pines. *I own the goddam sky.*

I passed a sign for "Rattlesnakes. Free. 2 mi." Passed the Green Frog Café, long abandoned, with a sign out front, "We Never Close."

A mile down the road a hand-lettered poster nailed to a tree said, "Catfish Bate." A hoot owl moaned from the limbs. Another ad, this one for a palm reader, informed me, "Your Footur Awates."

I checked a rough map I'd drawn based on Spider's recollections of distinctive junctions. It appeared I should take a left on the gravel path up ahead, through a dark oak stand. At a crossroads to my right I noticed a country store. Fresh-cut wood. A blue plastic tarp lay crumpled in the grass. The store looked as though it had been here a while but Spider hadn't mentioned it.

The gravel petered out, turning to dirt and twisted ivy. The foliage thickened. The sky dimmed further. Day became night and I had to use my headlights. About a quarter of a mile later I emerged onto thin pavement. I expected to see the Navasota River. Instead, I faced row after row of strawberry fields. Latino workers crouched in the greenery, croker sacks slung across their backs. In just a few days all this sweat and labor would be transformed into sweetly packaged produce (with an elf or a smiling green giant on the label) in the bins of Houston's stores.

Barbed-wire fences, tall as two-story houses, surrounded a state pen nearby, a brand-new facility next to a waste dump and a closed public school.

The soil was redder here than it had been in Paley. The river had to be close. Spider once mentioned an icehouse to me: "Used to be a old tavern, been there for ages, folks said Sam Houston, Jim Bowie and Davy Crockett stopped to rest there when it b'longed to the Texas Infantry—anyways, when I's a kid, my old man used to drink there with his buddies after a day sharecroppin'. He'd toggle me along and tell me to play out back while the fellas traded hoo-raws. I 'member I found a whole bunch of Indian arrowheads in the dirt there. And little animal bones."

If I could find that place I could locate the shack where Spider was born and discover what was left of his earliest juke joints.

A cantaloupe field sloped to the west. "Tasted like the Savior's sweet blood," Spider once said of the fruit.

The map said there ought to be a sawmill near here and the rusted remains of a cotton gin. I turned my Chrysler around and poked along a dirt road embroidered with scorched blackberry brambles. I heard rhythmic chanting. Closer now. Field hands belting out a work tune? A gospel chorus?

I stopped the car. I grabbed my notebook and portable cassette recorder off the warm plastic seat and pushed my way through the brambles. Thorns pricked my arms. A wooden sign stopped me short. "Keep Out," it said. A crude red swastika had been slathered across the base of the sign, the thick paint dripping past rusty nail heads.

I peered through the bushes. Crew-cut men in combat fatigues marched in formation brandishing dusty rifles. In a field behind them, pinewood targets—primitive representations of Black men with big bug-eyes—swayed from bent trees. Scattered smoke-swales drifted among the gently creaking limbs.

A whole new American century is dawning and *this* is where we are? I thought. Surely not. Surely not.

Voices inching near. Foul cigars. Two men strolling. I pressed to the ground.

"—buddy over in Mena, Arkansas making drops just inside Honduras. He can get us on. Damn good pay."

"What's the game?"

"Ordnance one way, poppy coming back."

"Hell, I don't know. I'll think on it. What would I tell Shirl?"

"Shit, Rusty, you could set her up in a nice place over in Baytown. Curtains in the kitchen. Rosy, air-freshened john. She don't need to know where her American Dream is coming from."

"She wouldn't believe it, anyway."

They laughed.

Quietly, I scrambled backwards out of the bushes. I wriggled down a broad slope and turned for my car.

Six goons stood around it, peering in the windows. Goons with guns. They spotted me. "Who are you? State your name!" one man shouted.

I squelched my impulse to run. They meant business and wouldn't hesitate to shoot me in the back.

"*Name*, asshole!"

"George Palmer."

The man snatched the notebook from my hands. "Goddammit, are you a reporter? What are you doing here?"

"No, no, I'm a . . . birdwatcher. Chasing a rare . . . bird." You idiot, I thought.

The fellow smelled of greasepaint. His face was a brilliant emerald color. His neck was as red and raw as rare flank steak. "Give me your wallet," he said. The others closed ranks around him. I noticed a welter of burns, some quite large, on most of their faces, arms and hands.

Insects popped like Bingo balls in the fields around us. The man pulled out my credit cards. "You better be who you say you are," he said. He studied my driver's license. "What did you see?"

"Nothing. I . . . nothing. Really."

Stale sweat. Beery breath. "All right. Go back to the city, you hear? We *kilt* all the damn birds."

He scattered my cards, my notebook and recorder on the ground. When I bent to pick them up, he kicked dirt in my eyes. "Get *out* of here!"

As I fishtailed down the road in my car, they peppered the air with bullets.

***

Oaks gave way to willows, willows to chalky hardscrabble. Wind flung grit against my windshield.

In the thirties and forties, in Mississippi, Klansmen harassed Alan Lomax for shaking Black men's hands in public or for calling them "mister." One night on Beale Street, as he was talking gospel with some harp players, he was startled to find himself suddenly surrounded by drawn pistols and a cop's twitchy flashlight.

I turned past a rolling burdock-ridge and glimpsed, for the first time, swelling blue water, muscled ripples. The Navasota.

Around a bend in the river, smoke huffed from the brick chimney of an unpainted shack. A cardboard sign on the door advertised "Hot Meat." Two Black kids, a boy and a girl, played on the porch.

A spicy-sweet sausage-smell hung in the trees. Up close, I saw that the children were playing with a pair of half-dead crawfish. The girl's dress was muddy and torn. Dried oats crusted the children's mouths. They didn't answer when I said hello.

Inside, a big man and two women stared at me. The space was tight. I maneuvered around a barrel and two broken fruit crates to reach the counter where the man stood. My steps shook the flooring. I smelled chicken sizzling somewhere.

"Howdy," I said.

The man nodded.

I unfolded my map. "I'm looking for—"

"Know nothin'," said the man.

"I think I'm—"

"Nothin' 'bout it."

The women disappeared behind a thin green curtain stretched across a doorway in back.

"I see," I said. "Old juke joint, closed now? 'The Honey Pot'?"

The man crossed his arms. A horsefly danced on rotting peaches in a bin.

"Okay," I said. I stuffed my map in my pocket. "Is there somewhere I can get gas, then?"

"'Bout six miles south." The man pointed.

Back on the porch, the little boy pulled the head off his crawfish.

***

A burned-out school bus sinking in a pool of ivy. A slender wooden cross by the road, wrapped in a mad tangle of dead roses.

I'd found the filling station. Another silent man.

I circled, reversed. Tracked and backtracked. The Thicket was aptly named.

The sky became a kaleidoscope, churning fury—by sundown it looked thicker than taffy, purple and black. Needling rain filled the tops of the trees.

"Fuck it," I said to my slapping wipers. I tossed my map out the window. How could I have been so stupid? My trip to the Delta two years ago, the dreary fast-food joints . . . that should have taught me the folly of my search. And of course blues culture had never been as romantic as I'd envisioned it. *Slavery*, for God's sake. Sharecropping.

In spite of all my notes, my interviews and articles, I didn't know a damn thing. Would I ever learn? They'd all tried to tell me: Lira, Mr. Thuot, Pedro. How could I possibly hope to know another race of people? It was hard enough to know Jean, Kelly, Alice. Myself.

I found a main road back to the interstate. Forget the blues, I thought. For now, at least. Think about food instead. Mounds of mashed potatoes. I was starving. Up ahead I saw a truck stop, a glary all-night restaurant.

Lord, I was tired.

Inside the restaurant I ducked into a smudgy phone booth by the kitchen. I checked my home machine. Alice had left a message. "George, hi. Sorry I've been hard to reach. I was a little under the weather." It surprised me how warm her voice made me feel. "No. That's not true," she said. "The truth is, Saturday felt . . . too fast, I guess. I'm sorry. I needed time to think about it all. Not just the sex, but the park, your world." She paused. I waited. "But anyway . . . I *would* like to see you again, if you haven't lost patience with me. Try and see what happens. So, I don't know . . . give me a call, okay? I'll be back at work tomorrow."

I stood cradling the receiver in my hands. Then I punched Paula's number.

"How's everybody?" I asked.

"Oh God, what a week it's going to be."

"I know you asked me to wait. But I'd *really* like to speak to the girls, if that's okay with you."

"George—"

"Please. Just for a sec. Let's not fight about it, okay?"

She sighed. "Hold on."

Elissa. "Hi, George."

"How you doing, cookie?"

"George, you know my friend Holly?"

I'd not met *any* of her friends in New Orleans. "Yes?"

"She's *very* vain."

170

"Really?" I'd never heard her use a grown-up word like "vain." Complex, layered, it sounded both funny and a little frightening in her tiny voice.

"Today while we were playing outside? She wouldn't take off her sweater even when it got *ninety degrees*!"

"I see."

"She just wanted to *look* good."

"And did she?"

This exasperated her. "Here's Jane," she said abruptly.

"George!"

"How are you, pumpkin?"

"I bumped my arm on the door. I'm much more better now."

"Good."

"But I cried a little this morning."

"I'm so sorry. Have you been practicing your play?"

"Some of the girls won't learn their lines."

"Hm. Can you be like the director, then, and tell them how important it is?"

"I guess."

"I think you'd be really good at it."

"Okay!"

I heard Paula call her to come wash up.

"Okay, honey. Sleep well tonight. I love you. Kiss your sister for me."

"*Ewww*!"

I'd save my next round with Paula for later this week.

Dizzy with hunger now I found a corner booth and ordered a chicken-fried steak. Truckers slurped coffee at the counter. "Don't know what it's like west of N'Awlins," one said. "I heard around mid-afternoon they had gale-force winds."

"Lotta shit in the road," said another.

"Just have to take my chances."

My steak arrived drowned in steaming white gravy. I picked up my fork. It weighed a hundred pounds. I must have dozed.

Next thing I knew my plate was gone, the ice had melted in my tea, and the check lay in a dribble of water on the table. The waitress, pale, with a scribbled nametag, "Sally," said, "Didn't know whether to shake you, partner, or let you be. You looked like you needed your beauty rest."

I rubbed my face. "Yes. I guess I did."

"Food got cold. I only charged you half. But I can bring you another if you like."

I didn't seem to be hungry anymore. Just bushed. "I appreciate it. No." I handed her a ten. "I should get on."

I stood in the parking lot letting the sharp air wake me up. The sky couldn't make up its mind. The wind tossed twigs across the road: a clicking sound like aspirin spilling from a bottle. In the car I tried my radio. An ousted former president of an obscure Latin American country told a reporter, "Not even the forces of history can move me." Then: slushy static. The silence made me realize I probably wouldn't see much of Spider anymore. He had more opportunities to play now and he was tired of white folks "slummin'." Like the other members of my families, he'd soon be gone from my life.

I switched on my lights and glimpsed an owl brooding in an oak tree by the road. I yawned, turned the car and wound on back to Mama Houston. I rolled down my window to smell the "goddam sky." If I didn't make it home too late, maybe I could walk the old woman to Carlos's restaurant.

Author's Note

I always intended *Tales from the Bayou City* to be a novel but, for various reasons, I wound up publishing sections of it as discrete short stories and never realized the fuller vision. A version of "Low Rider" appeared in the *New Yorker* and subsequently in my collection *The Woman in the Oil Field*. "Comfort Me With Apples," in different form, appeared in the *Southern Review* and won the Texas Institute of Letters Short Fiction Prize. It was later published in my collection *It Takes a Worried Man*, along with "Tombstone Television" and a radically different version of "Burying the Blues." I have now revised and regathered the pieces in their proper form.

I am indebted to Carl Lindahl, particularly to his book *Earnest Games: Folkloric Patterns in the Canterbury Tales*, for some of the ideas in "Low Rider." I am also grateful to Martha Grace Low, dear companion of those confused and dizzying days. She taught me what I knew about Houston, and so much more besides.

Other persons crucial to these tales: John McNamara and Cynthia Santos, and the late, great poets George Manner and Michelle Boisseau.

Thanks to Michelle Dotter of Dzanc Books. Thanks to Ghislain Viau for the splendid design. And my deep gratitude to Jim Gauer of Zerogram Press.